*'I wish it was possible to marry
you and live happily ever after.
But it isn't.'*

Holly sat up. 'I have to go.'

His comment had put a wedge between them.
Graham realised he'd spoken with that intent.
Don't stop her from leaving, he ordered himself.
But his hands operated on their own, reaching to
stroke her back. She shivered in response.

'Kiss me good-night?' he asked.

His heartbeat quickened with the moment's
suspense as she fought a losing battle within
herself. The fact that she didn't stand a chance of
winning it brought a fierce pleasure. He'd won
this battle, he thought, as she leaned down,
bringing her lips to his.

But would he win the war she waged against his
bachelorhood?

Dear Reader,

Welcome to Special Edition.

This month sees the final instalment of THE STOCKWELLS family saga—Jackie Merritt's *The Cattleman and the Virgin Heiress* allows the amnesia-afflicted Stockwell heiress to experience a very different kind of life...

How about catching the most eligible single dad in town? That's exactly what the heroine of Carole Halston's *Because of the Twins...* attempts to do in our THAT'S MY BABY! mini-series. Of course, another vastly eligible bachelor appears in Diana Palmer's SOLDIERS OF FORTUNE story, *The Last Mercenary*. Her ruggedly dangerous hero needs to deal with his past before he can claim his bride...

For all those who have been reading and enjoying the hugely successful MONTANA BRIDES, we have *And The Winner—Weds!* by Robin Wells which is connected to this series. Look out for *Just Pretending* next month.

Finally, we round off the month with Jean Brashear's super revenge story *Texas Royalty* and *Cowboy's Baby* by Victoria Pade—where a temporary shotgun marriage is beginning to look very permanent!

Enjoy!

The Editors

Because of the Twins...

CAROLE HALSTON

™ SILHOUETTE®
SPECIAL EDITION™

To my niece, Robin,
mother of adorable twins, Hunter and Justin.

*Silhouette, Silhouette Special Edition and Colophon are
registered trademarks of Harlequin Books S.A., used under licence.*

*First published in Great Britain 2002
Silhouette Books, Eton House, 18-24 Paradise Road,
Richmond, Surrey TW9 1SR*

© Carole Halston 2000

ISBN 0 373 24342 1

23-0502

*Printed and bound in Spain
by Litografía Rosés S.A., Barcelona*

CAROLE HALSTON

is a native of south Louisiana, where she lives with her sea-faring husband, Monty, in a rural area on the north shore of Lake Pontchartrain, near New Orleans. Her favourite pastime is reading, but she also gardens and plays tennis. She and Monty are camping enthusiasts and tow their twenty-six-foot mobile home to beautiful spots all over the United States.

Fans can write to Carole at PO Box 1095, Madisonville, LA 70447, USA.

Every month Silhouette Special Edition brings to you

That's my baby!

Sometimes bringing up baby can bring surprises... and showers of love!

Look out for:

May 2002

BECAUSE OF THE TWINS...
by Carole Halston

June 2002

MY LITTLE ONE
by Linda Randall Wisdom

July 2002

DADDY IN DEMAND
by Muriel Jensen

Chapter One

"Hello. Is anyone here?" called a woman's voice from the outer office. Then, in a more irritable tone she said, "*No,* Jennifer! Don't sit on the floor! Justin, hold on to Aunt Lena's hand!"

These instructions were met with childish whimpers of resistance, leading Graham to surmise that his visitor had a couple of small kids in tow. He got hurriedly to his feet and headed for the door. It was noon and his secretary, Angela, had gone to lunch. She was the mother of three and an expert on kids, so Graham relied on her to protect the premises from being trashed on those occasions—rare, but memorable—when a client brought his or her offspring along.

Graham was at a total loss when it came to dealing with children—an understandable deficiency, since he hadn't spent much time in the company of small fry. The younger of two boys, he'd grown up with virtually no contact with infants or toddlers. It was silly, but Graham regarded the whole notion of fatherhood as extremely intimidating, feelings he always owned up to when questioned on the subject by women he dated.

As he headed down the hall to the outer offices, he reflected on his unmarried state and wondered whether his candor on the subject of children had acted as a roadblock, preventing any of his romantic involvements from leading to marriage. He'd been thinking about this more and more since he'd turned thirty recently.

Only once had he proposed, more than four years ago. The words *"Will you marry me?"* had popped out in a moment of passion during his most intimate relationship.

He never dwelled on that memory, which still twinged.

"Can I help you?" he asked from the doorway to the outer office.

His unexpected visitor was a stranger, an attractive blond woman in her fifties who looked as harried as she'd sounded. Dressed smartly in a suit, she definitely wasn't your stereotypical doting aunt, but he assumed, since she'd referred to herself as

Aunt Lena, that the two preschool children with her must be her niece and nephew. Or, more likely, her great-niece and great-nephew. Both of them appeared to be unhappy campers, tugging to pull free of her firm grip on their small hands.

"Are you Graham Knight, the architect?" she inquired.

"Yes, I am—"

She'd turned her attention to the children. "Justin and Jennifer, will you *please* stand still? If you'll behave yourselves for five minutes, Aunt Lena will buy you an ice cream."

"I don't want an ice cream," Justin whined, tugging harder.

"Me, neither." Jennifer sank down on the carpet and proceeded to throw a tantrum, kicking the floor with her patent-leather shoes.

Graham didn't budge from the doorway. He had to raise his voice to be heard over the little girl's loud wailing. "Would you care to make an appointment?"

"What a fiasco!" His prospective client sighed. "I should have called you in advance or written a letter, I suppose. I'm Lena Booth." She had to shout, too, over the racket Jennifer was making. "Heather Booth's aunt. I believe you and Heather dated four or five years ago. You remember her?"

"Why, yes, I remember Heather well." She was the woman he'd proposed to, the woman who'd turned him down and broken off with him shortly afterward.

"Jennifer and Justin are Heather's children. They're twins."

Heather's children? Graham regarded the small girl and boy with new perspective, adjusting to their identity. Justin, brown-haired with brown eyes, didn't resemble his mother, but Jennifer had Heather's blond hair and blue eyes. She would probably be a pretty little girl if her face weren't contorted with the fit she was throwing.

"If I let you go, will you promise to behave for a few minutes while Aunt Lena has a conversation with Mr. Knight?" Lena Booth said, addressing her charges. "You can watch the pretty fish in the aquarium."

Jennifer promptly quieted, nodding.

"I'll be good," Justin mumbled sulkily.

When she had released their hands, the little boy walked over toward the aquarium, as prompted, but his sister sidled in the opposite direction, toward Angela's workstation. Graham watched her nervously.

"Heather never mentioned having an aunt who lived on the North Shore," he said to Lena Booth, taking for granted she would understand that he was referring to the North Shore of Lake Pontchartrain.

"I don't live in Louisiana. I live in Jackson, Mississippi. I drove here today specifically to meet you and introduce you to the twins.''

Graham frowned at her in puzzlement. Why the dickens did she think he would want to meet Heather's children? "Heather told you about me?''

"Oh, yes. I threatened to contact you much sooner, when she came back to Jackson pregnant and pleased as punch with herself. But I didn't. Now I wish I had. I regretted my mistake even more when I had you investigated recently and confirmed what a decent man you are. Justin, stop doing that! You'll scare the fish!''

Justin was slapping his palms on the glass front of the aquarium, making loud smacking sounds.

"Why contact me? And why on earth did you have me investigated?'' Graham asked in bafflement.

"You really don't have a clue, do you?'' She shook her head, her expression oddly pitying. "Do your math. The twins are three and a half years old. Add nine months and then backtrack in time. Jennifer, leave the computer alone!''

Graham glanced blindly over at the little girl, who was busy punching keys on Angela's keyboard. "Now wait just a minute!'' he exclaimed, wagging his hand at Lena Booth. "You're not trying to tell me—''

"I'm afraid so,'' she said simply. "Heather had her heart set on being a mom, but she didn't want the complication of a husband. Nor did she like the idea of using a sperm bank. She wanted to make sure she was getting sound genes for her child. She was planning on having one baby, mind you, not two.''

Graham clutched both sides of the doorframe, shaking his head from side to side in denial. It dawned on him that Heather's aunt was speaking of her niece with sadness as well as disapproval.

"Good God, has something *happened* to Heather?" he asked.

Lena nodded. "She was on vacation with the man she was dating. They'd gone to Italy. There was a terrible automobile accident. Neither of them survived."

Even in his state of shock and horror, Graham realized she'd carefully chosen her words so as not to state in the children's hearing that their mother had died.

"Poor kids," he murmured. "They've been told?"

"Yes. In euphemistic terms. They miss Heather, of course, but they spent most of their waking hours with a daytime nanny. As you can judge for yourself, they've been raised without any discipline."

Graham looked helplessly over at Jennifer, who was now busily pulling out drawers at Angela's workstation. Justin had stopped banging on the aquarium but had his face pressed against the glass, mouth open and tongue hanging out.

His kids? No way. There had to be some mistake. Please, God, let me wake up and discover this is a bad dream, Graham implored silently.

"Of course, you'll want some scientific proof," Lena stated, as though reading his panicky thoughts. "Especially if you were extremely careful and took precautions yourself during your affair with Heather."

Graham figured his sick expression told its own tale, but he elaborated, "She told me she was on the Pill. And showed me a recent lab report giving her a clean bill of health. She said she'd just taken out a work disability insurance policy that required her to prove she was disease-free."

"The part about the insurance policy was true."

"This is straight out of some bad movie! What the devil am I supposed to do?" Graham answered his own question before she could speak. "Naturally, I'll take financial responsibility. If it turns out I really was the sperm donor," he added in an undertone, so the children could not hear.

"Frankly, after seeing you face-to-face, I don't think there's much doubt. Have you looked closely at Justin? I'll bet you looked a lot like he does now when you were his age." She glanced over at her great-nephew, who'd lost interest in the aquarium and was now busy clearing a low table of the magazines neatly arranged on its surface. "For your mother's sake, I hope you were better behaved. Justin, don't throw the magazines on the floor! Just turn the pages gently and look at the pictures!"

"Justin," Graham said sternly.

Surprisingly the little boy raised his head, seeming to focus attention on Graham for the first time. Graham's heart sank as he gazed into a boyish face that was probably a replica of his own face when he was a youngster of three years and six months.

Once she saw that Justin was engaged in the task of restocking the magazines and was, like his sister, paying the adults in the room no mind, Lena confirmed in a low voice, "See what I mean?" Her tone held sympathy. "I'm really sorry my niece put you in this bind. In her defense, she never intended for you to be any the wiser."

"What she did was wrong! It was downright *immoral.*"

"I agree. And I would have informed you against her wishes that you were a father, but Heather convinced me not to. She insisted she wasn't cheating you by keeping you ignorant. She said she'd made sure in advance that you weren't one of those men who wanted a family."

"God..." Graham put both hands up to his head as though he could jump-start his numbed brain to come up with some magic solution. "Before you go, give me your address and phone number. We'll talk later, maybe tonight. I'll start sending you monthly checks.''

Her expression had turned pitying again. She glanced at the children, still busily playing, and said, ''Graham, I didn't come here today to get money for child support. I'm quite a well-to-do woman. Also very busy running a large corporation in Jackson. I can't take on raising Justin and Jennifer. I'm past the age of becoming a mom, and lack the patience. It wouldn't be fair to them.''

''Who's going to raise them? Heather's parents?''

''Obviously Heather never told you much about them or you wouldn't even suggest the idea. Mildred and Bill—Bill's my brother—divorced when Heather was three. She shuttled back and forth between them, poor darling. They're both on their third or fourth marriage now. It's hard to keep track. I won't go into the details except to say that Justin and Jennifer would be far better off in a good foster home than with either of their maternal grandparents.''

''A *foster* home! Isn't there another relative?''

''Not on Heather's side. There's a married cousin, Andy, who's stable, but he's currently living in a foreign country.'' She raised her eyebrows. ''Your parents perhaps?''

Graham immediately rejected that suggestion. ''My parents run a hardware store that they own in

Picayune, Mississippi. Plus they have their hobbies and interests. No way would I ask them to raise a couple of young kids at their stage in life. My brother is divorced.''

Lena made no reply, but just gazed at him sympathetically. Panic bloomed inside Graham at what she was surely considering as his only option.

''*I* can't raise them,'' he told her, pointing to himself. ''I'm single. And I know *nothing* about bringing up kids.''

Still she said nothing. The panic strengthened into an emotion more akin to terror.

''I live in a two-bedroom condo and use one of the bedrooms as my home study,'' he went on, presenting his case as if it would convince any reasonable person. ''There aren't any children living in the whole complex. It just wouldn't be a suitable environment. *I* would be a lousy father.''

''I'm not so sure about that. You might be the best thing that ever happened to Justin and Jennifer and, one would hope, vice versa.''

''Look at Jennifer!'' Justin shouted, chortling. Graham had been dimly aware that the little boy had completed his mission of throwing all the copies of *Architectural Digest* on the floor and had climbed up onto the sofa and was using it like a trampoline, jumping up and down.

''Jennifer, don't do that!'' scolded Lena as she rushed over to Justin's sister, who'd discovered Angela's plastic tube of hand cream. The little girl had removed the cap and was holding the tube aloft, upside down, squeezing out a long strand of cream.

The whole scene became surreal for Graham. It was beyond comprehension that he would be expected to deal with these two pint-size vandals. Supporting them financially was one thing, but take them home with him and turn them loose in his condo? "No way," he murmured in a tone of despair.

Lena wrested the tube from Jennifer's hands, and Graham braced himself for a howl, but Jennifer seemed satisfied with patting one small patent leather shoe in the blob of pink cream that had fallen to the carpet.

"That was very naughty, Jennifer."

"I'm not always naughty," the little girl said. "Mary says I can be a little angel sometimes."

"Mary was their daytime nanny," Lena explained to Graham.

"Can we go and have ice cream now?" Justin asked, leaping off the sofa. He ran over to his great-aunt.

"I thought you didn't want ice cream," she replied.

"I do! I want strawberry."

"I want vanilla with chocolate syrup and sprinkles," said Jennifer.

Graham suppressed a shudder at a vision of the

two of them with cups of ice cream at their disposal.

"Have you behaved yourselves well enough to deserve a treat?" Lena asked them.

"Jennifer was badder than me," Justin pointed out.

"No, I wasn't!"

Lena took each of them by the hand. "Come over closer to this nice man Aunt Lena has been talking to. He's someone very important."

"Who is he?" asked Justin.

"He's your daddy."

"Our daddy?" Jennifer questioned skeptically. "We don't have a daddy. We just have a mommy, but she's in heaven now."

Graham had gone as still as a statue. The sense of unreality was more pronounced than ever. Lena, flanked by the two children, approached him.

"Are you really our daddy?" Justin asked when they'd come to a standstill.

Words wouldn't come out of Graham's mouth. He had to swallow. "Yes, Justin, I believe I am."

"We grew in our mommy's stomach," Jennifer informed him, obviously still not putting much stock in his paternity claim.

"I was borned first." Justin stood very straight. "I'm taller than Jennifer."

"And he has a penis. I don't."

"Maybe you children would like to give your daddy a hug or a kiss," Lena suggested.

"I'm a total stranger to them," Graham protested.

Jennifer and Justin gazed up into his face. From their expressions they were processing the idea.

"He's too tall," the little girl pointed out.

Graham felt like a robot as he lowered himself to a squatting position. Jennifer moved first and Justin followed her lead. They pressed their lips to his cheeks.

"Give them a hug, why don't you?" Lena prompted, and he complied in a gingerly fashion. "That's nice." She sighed with satisfaction. "Now, why don't the four of us go out for ice cream? Then I'll be on my way back to Jackson."

Graham stood up, alarm bells going off at her use of the singular pronoun. "You're taking the twins back, too, aren't you? I need some time to make arrangements. And you'll need to pack up their clothing and toys."

"I have several big suitcases in the trunk of my car. I'll send the rest right away. Let's go, kids." She clapped her hands briskly. "Aunt Lena needs to be on the road in forty-five minutes."

Graham accompanied them, leaving his outer office in total shambles. His mind and emotions were in a similar state of disruption. His life had just gone from sane and orderly to crazy and chaotic.

Chapter Two

"Holly, isn't this a fabulous turnout!" gloated Ann Johnson, the president of the North Shore Businesswomen Club. "Everyone who bought a raffle ticket must have showed up for the cocktail party and drawing tonight."

"Not quite everyone," Holly replied. "I counted the invitation cards I collected at the door. A hundred and seventy-four, and we sold two hundred tickets."

"At $250 each! That's $50,000, less expenses, for our scholarship fund." Ann toasted Holly with her champagne glass. "Here's to you for coming up with the idea for this year's fund-raiser. It was

sheer genius to tap into our members' expertise and
hold a raffle with multiple prizes like Decorating
Consultant for a Week, Girl Friday for a Week,
Nanny for a Week. Our ticket buyers loved the novelty of taking a chance on free service by an expert.
And at $250, our raffle winners will be getting real
bargains.''

''The only glitch was that those who bought tickets from me all had their favorite prize they hoped
to win.''

''Same here. A couple of bachelors pointed out
they wouldn't have any use whatever for a nanny.
But they were good sports when I explained that
we weren't selling separate tickets. It would be luck
of the draw as to who won what.'' Ann glanced
around, searching the crowd of well-dressed people
sipping drinks and munching on canapés. ''One of
my bachelor ticket buyers was Graham Knight. I
don't see him, and he said he wouldn't think of
missing what he called our 'annual bash.'''

''No, he's not here.'' Holly sipped her champagne.

''You've already noticed our handsome architect's absence.'' Ann pointed out the obvious, her
smile teasing. ''Do I detect disappointment?''

''If you do, I must be fond of rejection.'' Holly's
tone was wry.

''You? Rejected by a red-blooded male? That's
hard to imagine, especially as gorgeous as you look

tonight. I love your emerald-green outfit. Oh, Gina's signaling us. It's time to hold the raffle." The club president hurried off.

Holly sighed glumly, touching the shimmering green silk of her dinner suit before she followed in Ann's wake. The dinner suit was new. She'd bought it especially to wear tonight. Darn it, she'd wanted to look her most "gorgeous" because she expected Graham Knight to be at the fund-raiser party.

A week ago she'd encountered him in the supermarket, of all places, and they'd chatted briefly. The chemistry had sizzled between them, as usual. Holly had bitten her tongue to keep from asking, "Are you busy tonight?" A modern woman, she rejected the old rules that required a guy to ask a woman out and never vice versa. That was nonsense, in her opinion. But Graham had already refused her once before during the past year, when they were working together on a job for a builder. Graham had been the architect and Holly the interior decorator.

So she hadn't tried to make a date with him in the supermarket. Neither had he tried to make a date with her. But in parting he had referred casually to seeing her at the fund-raiser party. Darn it, Holly *was* disappointed he hadn't come.

Which meant she actually must be fond of rejection. Except that all her instincts as a woman told her Graham Knight was every bit as attracted to her as she was to him. What was his hang-up where she was concerned?

The next time I get the chance, I'm going to ask him, Holly promised herself.

The North Shore Businesswomen Club had booked a banquet room at a local hotel for tonight's party and raffle. A station for the drawing had been set up in advance on a dais at one end of the room. On a draped table sat an elegant flower arrangement, compliments of a florist member, but the focal point of attention as the guests gathered around the dais were two crystal bowls flanking the centerpiece, one containing five small envelopes and the other containing two hundred envelopes of a comparable size.

After a speech, Ann proceeded with the raffle by first introducing the five club members who were either donating their services or that of an employee as prizes. Holly was among them. She would be donating her own skills for the Decorating Consultant for a Week prize.

Next, Ann called for a volunteer to step up and draw two envelopes, one from either bowl. A jovial bald-headed man responded. He first read out the name of the winner, a woman who was present. After the excitement had died down, he revealed her prize in his booming voice, "Nanny for a Week!"

The raffle proceeded with three more volunteers assisting. In order, lucky ticket buyers won Fashion Consultant for a Week, Personal Fitness Trainer for a Week and Girl Friday for a Week. Finally, only one prize envelope remained to be awarded to the winner of Decorating Consultant for a Week.

Holly smiled at her own reaction. Her nerves had tightened with the suspense. Who would win her?

The last volunteer, a matron in pearls who happened to be one of Holly's wealthier clients, stepped up beside Ann. Holly had sold Gwendolyn Myers her fund-raiser ticket. Gwendolyn dipped a manicured hand into the bowl still filled with envelopes, fished around at length to prolong the drama and eventually plucked out one. Careful of her nails, she opened the envelope and showed the card inside it to Ann, who blinked and cast Holly a surprised look that said, *You won't believe this.*

"Shall I read the name?" asked Gwendolyn, getting into her role as though she were an emcee on an awards program.

"Please do," said Ann, whose expression was amused.

Somebody, read the blasted name, thought Holly, her curiosity thoroughly aroused.

Gwendolyn cleared her throat and intoned, "The final lucky winner of the evening is...Graham Knight."

Holly's mouth fell open.

"Is he present tonight?" Gwendolyn was inquiring.

"No, I don't believe Graham was able to come," Ann spoke up smoothly. She moved things along and concluded the raffle with another speech while Holly was adjusting to this unexpected development.

"Holly, will you notify Graham Knight? Or would you like for me to?"

"I'll do it," Holly replied without hesitation. She and Ann were on their way to their cars and had paused in the parking lot. "I won't mind having a legitimate excuse to pay him a visit at his office. You probably guessed that from our earlier conversation when his name came up."

"True," Ann admitted laughingly. "What a coincidence for him to win you!"

"How well do you know Graham, if you don't mind my asking?"

"Fairly well. Our connection, of course, is Bob." Bob was Ann's husband, a prominent builder on the North Shore. "We've had Graham over to dinner at our house quite a few times over the past five years. Bob considers him an excellent architect and is always glad to land a project designed by Graham."

"When he came to dinner, did he bring a date?" Holly was blatantly fishing for information.

"On a couple of occasions he brought a very striking woman he was obviously quite infatuated with. As a matter of fact, she had coloring very similar to yours. Golden-blond hair and blue eyes. And I believe she was an interior decorator, too. Her name has slipped my mind. We're talking at least four years ago."

"Hmm, I wonder if she's still around. I haven't run into any other decorators who look like me."

"The relationship apparently didn't last. Maybe she moved away. It's my impression that Graham hasn't been that involved with anyone since. When I quiz him, he always denies having a special woman in his life. He's such a nice solid guy. I've no doubt he's good husband material."

"I'm not looking for a husband," Holly volunteered frankly. "But I enjoy male company, and he's awfully likable and cute."

Ann lightly slapped her forehead. "A brain cell just kicked in! Heather. That was Graham's woman friend's name. Heather. Holly. Same first initial," she remarked.

Holly wasn't acquainted with anyone named Heather.

The two women bade one another good-night. On the way home Holly mulled over the background on Graham's past love life that Ann had divulged. Maybe he was still carrying a torch for this old girlfriend Heather who bore some outward resemblance to Holly. Maybe he was reminded of Heather everytime he ran into Holly and experienced nostalgia or pain.

It would explain why he kept his distance from Holly when he plainly was drawn to her.

One way or another, Holly intended to solve the mystery. Darn, she wished tomorrow were a weekday instead of Saturday. She guessed she would have to wait until Monday to drop in on Graham at his office and make her announcement. "You lucky man, you won me!"

By then he might have heard through the grapevine. Holly liked the idea of breaking the news personally. It was rather late in the evening for someone—including her—to phone him tonight. She was probably safe. What the heck, Holly thought, I'll call him tomorrow morning at home and ask him to meet me for coffee.

Graham's home number was conveniently listed in the phone directory.

Holly waited until nine-thirty to call, figuring that was a decent time to bother him on a Saturday. If she waited too late, she increased her chances of not catching him at home before he went out to run errands or whatever.

He picked up on the second ring and said hello in a tone that was almost a shout. Holly could hear some kind of loud background noise. A TV play-ing?

"Hi, Graham. This is Holly Beaumont. I have some news I'd like to tell you in person. How about meeting me for coffee at the Breakfast Joint?"

"I wish," he said with an emotion that seemed to be bitterness.

Were those the voices of children shrieking and wailing?

"Graham, what's all that racket?"

"What? I can't hear you, Holly."

"I said what's all that racket?" she shouted. "Can't you turn the TV lower?"

"Hold on. I'll have to do it manually."

"Don't you have a remote?"

"God knows where it is, or whether it's still functioning. Hold on," he said again.

About ten seconds later some of the noise sub-sided, but not the shrieking and wailing. That noise obviously wasn't coming from the TV.

"Okay. That's a little better," he said. "Look, Holly, I'm sorry, but I'm tied up here. Justin, don't hit your sister. Jennifer, stop kicking Justin." His pleas, obviously not intended for her ears, held des-peration.

"Whose children are those?" Holly asked, hav-ing deduced that he was addressing a couple of kids.

"Mine." The bitterness again.

"Yours? I didn't know you were a father."

"Neither did I until yesterday."

"How old are they?" Holly was as fascinated as she was astonished.

"Three and a half. They're twins—a girl and a boy."

"Is their mother there, too?" She hadn't heard a woman speaking.

"No, she's deceased. I learned that yesterday, too, from the great-aunt who delivered the children."

"'Delivered' them? You mean she just brought them and left them?"

"You got it."

"Graham, this is the most bizarre story I've ever heard!" Holly exclaimed.

"Tell me about it. Sorry to be abrupt, but I'd better hang up before these two hurt each other." He said a terse goodbye and cut the connection.

"Poor guy!" she sympathized out loud. "What a predicament!" Holly sat there a few moments, flooded with sympathy and trying to imagine what it would feel like to be in his shoes. One minute a single man with only himself to worry about and the next minute a daddy with twins.

Graham had come across as desperate and downright depressed, understandably. His life had been thrown into a turmoil and he didn't seem to be coping very well. It would be criminal of Holly to go about her business today and not play Good Samaritan, especially since she'd had quite a bit of experience dealing with children during her teenage years. Baby-sitting had been her main source of extra spending money.

I'll go over to Graham's place and help him out for a few hours, Holly decided.

Generosity was her main motivation, but she was also dying of curiosity to meet his offspring!

The decision made, Holly briefly considered calling Graham back and alerting him that he should expect her. Then she scratched that plan and decided simply to appear at his door. Fortunately, she'd been inquisitive enough to note his address when she was stuffing raffle ticket stubs into envelopes for the drawing.

The drive from her house in the village of Madisonville to Graham's condo near the lake in Mandeville took Holly between fifteen and twenty minutes. At ten o'clock she was ringing his doorbell.

Graham jerked the door open in midact of shoving his free hand through dark brown hair that already was rumpled. He wore a T-shirt tucked into his unbelted jeans, and athletic shoes. Despite the dark circles under his eyes that suggested he hadn't slept well, despite his harried expression, Holly found him as ruggedly good-looking as ever.

"Holly," he said blankly. His gaze took in her

jeans and T-shirt and athletic shoes. Holly's body hummed pleasurably in response to his inspection, the way it always did when she was around him.

"Hi. I came to give you some moral support," she announced cheerfully. "On the phone you sounded pretty rattled."

"This is hell." He rubbed his forehead roughly with his palm. "Sheer hell."

"The TV's been turned up loud again," Holly observed. She could hear the soundtrack of a cartoon show blaring inside the condo.

"They insist on playing it loud enough to burst their eardrums. When I turn it down, they turn it back up again."

"Did you try taking away the remote?"

"Yes. I tried that," he confirmed wearily. "But they scream and yell like a couple of banshees when they don't get their way. I'm afraid the neighbors will call the police. So I gave the remote back to them to shut them up.

"God, you should see the inside of my condo. It looks like vandals have struck. I was cleaning up the kitchen when you rang the doorbell. Cereal and milk all over the place. Broken dishes. These two kids are monsters disguised as children, Holly. Monsters."

"Can I come in? I'll give you a hand with the kitchen."

He hesitated before saying, "Sure. But enter at your own risk."

Even in a state of emergency he had his qualms about admitting her into his condo. Holly ignored her little stab of hurt for the time being. She smiled and stepped inside the foyer, commenting, "Three-and-a-half-year-olds can't be *that* dangerous."

The trained decorator in her automatically noticed and approved the décor of his condo. Mexican tile floor in the foyer gave way to oatmeal-colored carpet in the living area. Soft white walls, striking artwork, glove-soft brown leather upholstery, natural finishes on wooden furniture. Tasteful, comfortable, and masculine.

It was an adult environment. The toys strewn about the living room looked totally out of place as did the two children lying on their stomachs in front of a thirty-six-inch TV housed in a handsome built-in entertainment center. Doors in the entertainment center stood open, drawers were pulled out, video-tapes and CDs had been tossed about helter-skelter.

"See what I mean about vandals?" Graham gestured helplessly. "I tried to tell them that I didn't own any videos or CDs for kids, but they refused to listen."

"You mind if I ask them to turn the TV down?" she asked.

"You're wasting your breath. But go ahead."

Holly walked over to the twins and clapped her

hands together smartly to attract their attention. "Justin. Jennifer. The TV's too loud," she said. The children looked up at her, taking her measure. It was difficult for Holly to maintain her brisk manner as she gazed into their faces. They were both adorable, the blue-eyed, fair-haired little girl and the brown-haired, brown-eyed little Graham lookalike. "I said, 'The TV's too loud.' It hurts our ears. Turn the volume down." She mimicked using an imaginary remote control.

Justin held the real remote clutched in both hands. After long seconds of deliberation, he pressed a small finger on the appropriate button.

"Well, I'll be d—" Graham muttered. He'd followed behind her but stopped a few yards away.

"Lower than that, please," Holly directed Justin. She smiled at the little boy when he'd reluctantly obeyed. "Thank you. That's much better. And much safer. Loud noise can damage our eardrums and eventually make us deaf. That's why workmen running noisy machines wear ear protection."

"Who are you?" demanded Jennifer, sitting up.

"I'm Holly Beaumont, a friend of your daddy's."

The little girl's face clouded up and her bottom lip trembled. "He's not our daddy. Our mommy told us we didn't have a daddy, and I don't like him." Tears suddenly welled up, and Jennifer began to cry brokenheartedly. "I w-want my m-mommy to come b-back from heaven. I want to go to my h-house and stay with Mary.''

"Don't cry, sweetie," Holly crooned. Her own eyes wet, she sank down beside the distraught child and hugged her.

"I want Mommy to come back. And I want to go to my house," Justin said, breaking down and sobbing just as pitifully.

Holly gathered him close, too, and murmured reassurances that seemed woefully inadequate in light of the children's great loss. "Mommy wouldn't want you to cry like this. She would want you to be happy children. Tell you what. Let's dry those tears and do something really fun. Okay? How would you like for your daddy and me to take you to a playground?''

Graham had come closer. At his muffled sound of protest, Holly glanced up at him and read panic on his face. He shook his head hard and mouthed, "No way."

"Why not?" she mouthed back.

"You haven't ridden with them in a car," he said in an urgent undertone. "They won't keep their seat belts fastened. And if you let go of their hands when you're out in public, they can be gone in a flash. In different directions.''

He obviously spoke from terrifying experience.

"There're two of us. We can manage," Holly said confidently.

Meanwhile the children's sobs had quieted.

"A playground?" questioned Justin with interest, sniffling.

"With seesaws and swings?" Jennifer asked, wiping her wet little cheeks with her palms.

Holly looked pleadingly at Graham, who sighed in capitulation.

"Against all my better judgment," he said.

Chapter Three

"We can take my minivan," Holly offered, and Graham readily agreed once he'd determined she had child-safety locks on the back doors.

The two vehicles parked in his garage were a small extended-cab pickup and a sporty two-door car. Presumably he used the truck to drive to construction sites and the car for personal use. Holly tactfully didn't point out that neither qualified as a family automobile.

"This is like my mommy's minivan," Jennifer said as she scrambled up onto the middle bench seat after Holly had cleared it of decorating paraphernalia.

Justin climbed up beside his sister, elaborating on her statement. "Mommy's is green, too. And has wallpaper books and stuff in the back, like yours does."

"We ride in it to Grandma's house."

Their use of present tense brought on another wave of sadness that they'd been visited by tragedy at such a young age, but Holly shoved the emotion aside in the interest of being upbeat for their benefit. Justin's reference to wallpaper books in his mommy's minivan fed her curiosity. Was their mother the interior decorator named Heather whom Ann had described last night?

The picture of cooperative children, the twins assisted Holly as she buckled their seat belts for them. Graham stood back and watched, tense and seemingly prepared for them to bolt.

"You made that look easy," he said when she'd stepped out of the van and slid the door closed. "Yesterday it was a fifteen-minute battle getting them buckled in. And all for naught. They'd unbuckled themselves by the time I'd started the car. It took an hour to get home from my office by the time I pulled over four or five times. Finally I just gave up and drove as slowly and carefully as possible and prayed I wouldn't meet a policeman."

"No wonder you didn't want to take them to the park after an ordeal like that." Holly touched his arm in sympathy. He jerked away as though her hand had burned him.

"What *is* your problem with me?" she asked in exasperation.

"When are we going to the playground?" Justin called out, and Jennifer repeated his query with childish impatience.

"Right now," Holly replied, but she didn't budge. She was waiting for Graham to answer her.

"Sorry, I guess I'm a little on edge," he said, not quite meeting her eyes. "We'd better go before they get restless."

"Eventually I'd like an honest explanation," she informed him. "Because you've been 'on edge' around me long before the twins showed up."

He nodded soberly, not pretending to be mystified by her words. "Fair enough."

On the ride to a park near the Mandeville city hall, the children chattered about trips to a playground in Jackson with their nanny, Mary. There was no mention of any such outings with their mother, Holly noted.

"I'll hold Holly's hand," Jennifer announced, unsnapping her seat belt on arrival. She'd made a point earlier of refusing to take Graham's hand when they were exiting his condo.

"I'll hold my daddy's hand," Justin offered, as he had also done earlier.

"He's not our daddy. And I don't want to live at his house."

Graham said nothing, leaving it up to Holly to assume the role of adult in charge.

"Since you both were so well behaved on the drive here, I think you can be trusted to walk on your own," she said.

Her words gained her a horrified look from Graham. *Relax. It'll be okay,* she soothed him silently, not daring to reach out and give him a reassuring pat.

He did relax his vigilance ever so slightly as they trooped toward the playground equipment, Jennifer and Justin talking excitedly and hopping and skipping along like normal preschool children.

"Will you swing me, Holly?" Jennifer asked.

"Sure."

"My daddy can swing me," Justin said, going along with the adult assignments.

Holly found the little boy's readiness to accept a newfound daddy very sweet and endearing. So far he hadn't addressed Graham as Daddy in her hearing, but she suspected it wouldn't require much coaching for him to do so.

For the first half hour, the twins demanded close attention and constant supervising. Then half a dozen more children appeared, accompanied by parents. Jennifer and Justin began to interact with their potential playmates, Justin more so than Jennifer. Holly seized her opportunity to carry on private conversation with Graham, who continued to watch his children with hawklike intensity.

"Who is their mother?" she asked.

"A woman I dated named Heather Booth."

"Heather *Booth?*" Not only did Heather and Holly share the same first initial, but the same last initial, too, since Holly's surname was Beaumont!

Graham eyed her questioningly. "You knew her?"

"No. Ann Johnson mentioned her last night. At the fund-raiser party you didn't attend."

"I couldn't get a sitter on such short notice. Plus I was too shell-shocked to go out among people and be sociable."

"That's understandable." Once again Holly suppressed the urge to comfort him physically with a squeeze or a pat. It came naturally to her to be a demonstrative type of person. "You said on the phone that you didn't know you were a father until yesterday," she prompted.

"No, I didn't have the first suspicion that Heather had used me for a sperm donor." His tone was bitter. "Looking back, all the pieces fit. Now it makes sense that she broke off with me so suddenly. She'd accomplished her goal and gotten pregnant."

"Did she move away from the North Shore?"

Otherwise he might have kept tabs on her and known she'd become a mother.

He nodded. "She moved back to Jackson, Mississippi, where she was from. According to her aunt, Heather had given herself a six-month leave from her highly successful interior decorating business. Heather had lied and told me she was from north Louisiana."

"She didn't want you to be able to look her up."

"You got it," he said flatly.

"I wonder how she happened to pick the North Shore as the place to..." Holly's voice drifted off.

"The place to find just the right dumb male? I asked Lena Booth about that. She said Heather made trips to New Orleans for business and pleasure and was familiar with the population makeup of the North Shore."

Holly elaborated for herself, "Lots of well-educated young professionals, making up a good gene pool. Upscale, friendly environment. Where did you meet her?"

"At my health club. She introduced herself to me."

"Perfect." It was easy to understand how a woman would notice him working out in gym shorts and a T-shirt.

"Yeah, perfect."

"Don't misunderstand me," Holly hastened to say. "I don't at all approve of what Heather did. I think it was horribly immoral.'' She remembered Ann's words. *On a couple of occasions he brought a very striking woman he was obviously quite infatuated with.* ''You must have liked her a lot if the two of you became that intimate.''

''I more than 'liked' her. I asked her to marry me.''

''Oh, no. You poor guy.'' They were standing side by side. Before she could stop herself, Holly impulsively slipped her arm around his waist to give him a consoling hug. He stiffened. ''There you go again!'' she exclaimed, stung by his reaction. ''For heaven's sake, I was just showing sympathy, not trying to come on to you!''

''I don't deserve sympathy for being stupid. If I'd had any sense, I'd have taken precautions instead of trusting Heather when she pretended to be on birth-control pills.''

Holly wasn't about to be sidetracked. She was ready for an explanation of his behavior toward her. ''Do I remind you of Heather? Has that been the problem all along?'' She ticked off points on her fingers. ''Same initials. Both of us interior decorators. Maybe some similarity in looks, too?''

Graham sighed, running his right palm roughly down the back of his neck. ''I did a double take the first time I saw you from a distance. For one crazy second I thought you were Heather.'' His gaze took in her hair and face and wandered lower, arousing the pleasurable tingles of awareness. "But it's not just the hair color and eyes and...figure. You're so much like her in other ways."

"Could you be more specific?" Holly wasn't flattered, not after the insight into Heather's character she'd just gotten.

"No offense, but you're not exactly shy, and neither was she. The day we met, you asked me out on a date."

"I liked you. I sensed that the attraction was mutual. You didn't make the first move." Holly shrugged. Intuition suddenly struck her. "Heather asked you out on a date when you met her, I'll bet. And you accepted."

"Fool that I was, I found her boldness a refreshing change." His bitterness had resurfaced with recollection.

"Take my word for it. I would *never* sleep with a guy to get pregnant, and keep him ignorant of the fact. If I ever decide to be a single mother, I'll go the sperm bank route."

"If you 'decide.' It's something you've considered?"

"Yes," she admitted. "I love children, but I also love my career."

"What's wrong with getting married and having children the old-fashioned way so they have a mother and a father?"

"Great in theory. But marriage is a bigger long

shot for me than for your average person. I have a divorce gene on both sides of my family tree. Not only my parents but also all my aunts and uncles are on their third or fourth marriages. I tend to believe a child is better off in a stable home with one parent than being shuttled back and forth.''

He shook his head in disbelief. ''Your background is even similar to Heather's.''

''But I am *not* devious and manipulative,'' Holly stated.

The twins chose that moment to interrupt.

''I'm hungry!'' Jennifer announced, running up to Holly.

Justin was close behind his sister. ''Me, too! I want a hamburger and French fries!''

''I want chicken nuggets and French fries!

''Let's check with your daddy,'' Holly said, looking to Graham for a response. After all, he was the parent.

''Fast food?'' he said, frowning. ''Shouldn't kids their age eat a healthy diet?''

''Most of the time. But fast food occasionally is probably okay, don't you think?''

The twins were jumping up and down and clamoring for a kiddy's meal from their favorite franchise.

''Okay. Okay,'' Graham said, succumbing to the pressure. ''But they'll drink milk, not cola.''

In the parking lot, Justin climbed up into the minivan ahead of his sister, announcing, "It's my turn to sit by the window."

"No it's *not* your turn!" Jennifer shouted. She began to wail at the top of her lungs and stubbornly refused to climb up next to him.

He refused to yield his place.

Half-amused, Holly turned to Graham, who looked mortified. "How do we resolve this dispute?"

He lifted his hands in a helpless gesture, then spoke to his son, "Justin, why don't you let your sister sit there? She's a little girl."

"Now wait just a minute," Holly objected, hands on hips. "That's very sexist and not fair to Justin. Being a little girl doesn't mean Jennifer should have her way every time she makes a fuss."

"You're right." He spoke to his daughter, "Jennifer, please get into the van so that we can go and buy our lunch. It's a short ride."

"She can sit here," Justin said, and scooted over. Jennifer's wails instantly quieted. She promptly seated herself in the place he'd vacated.

"Thank you, Justin," Graham said.

When it was clear he intended to leave the matter there, Holly spoke up firmly. "When we come out of the restaurant, Justin will sit by the window on the ride home. Is that understood, Jennifer?"

"Come out of the restaurant?" Graham repeated,

his tone appalled. "You're intending to take them inside to eat?"

"Isn't that what you intended?"

"No, I figured we'd take the food home and contend with the mess there."

Both children had been following the exchange between the adults. They chimed in, begging to go inside the restaurant and play in the children's amusement center.

Once again Graham gave in. "Okay, okay," he said.

Holly could guess from his expression that he'd never before in his life felt any less enthusiasm for a meal out.

"Isn't that sweet? The little darlings fell sound asleep in front of the TV." Holly's tender smile lingered on her lips as she looked over at Graham. After returning to his condo, the adults had gone into the kitchen to clean up the mess made at breakfast. Finished, they'd come out into the living room and found the twins napping on the floor.

Lunch at the fast-food restaurant had undoubtedly proved to be about as bad as Graham had expected. Jennifer and Justin had managed to spill their cartons of milk and also knock over Holly's iced tea during the course of the meal. The iced tea had emptied right onto the crotch of Graham's jeans. Both twins had gotten ketchup smeared all over their faces and their clothes. They'd seemed to drop more fries on the floor than they'd succeeded in eating. Jennifer had sneezed with her mouth full of food, and Justin had choked on a bite of hamburger.

On the way out of the restaurant, Graham had apologized profusely to the woman who was wiping tables and tidying up. He'd no doubt made her day when he tipped her five dollars.

"Should I put them in bed?" Graham asked now, gazing at his children with his air of tense bewilderment. "I hate to wake them up."

"They seem comfortable lying on the carpet." Each twin had garnered a throw pillow. "Why not let them finish out their nap? I should probably go and let you grab one yourself. You look tired." Holly's tone was sympathetic.

"I am tired," he admitted. "But it's as much mental fatigue as anything else. I just can't believe I got myself into this dilemma. But I have." He glanced at the sleeping twins, compassion on his face. "I feel bad for them, too. They deserve a couple of good parents. Instead they end up with a totally inadequate father."

"Not inadequate. Just inexperienced."

"Inadequate," he insisted grimly. "I always suspected I wasn't cut out for parenthood, and now I realize I was right."

"Could we have a cup of coffee?" Holly asked.

He probably needed to talk out his fears and vent his emotions as much as he needed physical rest, and she was more than happy to stick around and serve as his sounding board.

"Sure. The least I can do is serve you coffee. You've helped me get through part of today."

He led the way back into the kitchen. Holly made herself comfortable at the table in the dining nook while he measured coffee and started the coffeemaker.

"Have you definitely decided to raise the twins yourself?" she asked.

"So far I haven't come up with any viable alternatives. I can't dump a couple of kids on my parents. Heather's parents have declined."

"There're no other family members on either side who would jump at the chance to give Justin and Jennifer a good home?"

"Not on my side. My brother, Greg, is divorced. Heather was an only child."

Another similarity, Holly reflected. She was also an only child.

Graham was continuing. "According to Lena Booth, the aunt, there's one married male cousin who might have agreed to adopt the twins. Apparently he and his wife want a family and haven't been able to have children. But he works for a major oil company and is currently living in Malaysia."

"Scratch him off."

Holly watched as he took down mugs from a cabinet, noting with pleasure the play of his T-shirt across broad shoulders and taut back muscles. From the waist down he didn't have anything to apologize for, either. He'd changed into clean jeans when they got back here after lunch. This pair fit perfectly, too.

"Do you take creamer? Sugar? Sugar substitute?" He glanced around and caught her admiring his body.

She jerked her gaze up to meet his and smiled sheepishly. "Just creamer, please."

He turned to face her, folding his arms across his chest. "Holly, I've got enough on my plate as it is."

Holly raised her eyebrows at his stern tone of reprisal. "I like the way you're built. What's the big deal?" she said lightly.

"I'm not about to get involved with you. Especially not now. That's the big deal."

This latest rejection hurt more than earlier ones had. The few hours in his company had somehow made her more vulnerable. "Ouch."

"I'm sorry to have to be so blunt."

"Tell me I'm not imagining things. The attraction is mutual, isn't it?"

"Don't play games. Of course I'm attracted to you."

"But you're convinced I'm too much like Heather for you to let down your guard."

He sucked in a deep breath and nodded.

"So are we having coffee or is that too risky?"

"Don't be flip," he said angrily.

"Would you rather I showed my disappointment?" Heather stood up. "Goodbye, Graham."

"Look, I'm sorry."

"Me, too."

Holly left. What more was there to say? For all her agitation, she was careful to close the door behind her very quietly so as not to disturb the sleeping twins.

"Where did Holly go?" Jennifer asked tearfully.

"She went home to her place," Graham answered.

"Is she coming back?" Justin asked, his brown eyes solemn.

"No, she isn't coming back." Graham sighed, empathizing with his children's downcast expressions. He couldn't blame Jennifer and Justin for objecting to Holly's absence after they awoke from their nap. Now they were stuck with him to take care of their needs.

"Why did she leave?" the little boy wanted to know.

Graham searched for an honest explanation they could comprehend. "Holly and I know each other through our work, but we aren't friends. We don't normally spend time together on weekends.''

''I want Holly,'' Jennifer said, beginning to sob.

''Please don't cry, Jennifer.'' Feeling more inept than he'd ever felt in his life, Graham crouched down near his little daughter, wanting to comfort her. She turned her back to him and scooted away beyond his reach.

''I want Holly! I want my mommy!'' she sobbed.

Justin crawled over near his twin and put his arms around her. Jennifer leaned into him, crying pitifully. They made a woebegone picture. Graham felt tears of compassion smarting his eyes.

''Would you like to watch TV?'' he suggested, hearing his desperation in his voice.

''Would you, sis?'' asked Justin, patting her on the back. ''You can hold the remote and change the channels.''

Jennifer sniffled and sat apart. Without looking at Graham she said to him, ''Can we have cookies and milk?''

''I don't have any cookies. But I have some crackers and cheese. You can come into the kitchen and eat a snack.''

She folded her small arms across her chest in a defiant stance. ''Mary lets us eat our snacks in the living room while we watch TV.''

Graham had a sudden vision of the restaurant where they'd created a scene of devastation. French fries scattered over the floor, table streaked with milk and ketchup, a pile of sodden napkins used to wipe up spillage.

He could easily imagine the mess the twins would make of his living room carpet if he humored Jennifer and gave them their snack in front of the TV. But maybe he should humor her to try to make friends. After all, a carpet could be cleaned. On the other hand, shouldn't there be house rules?

Hell, Graham didn't know what he should do.

Halfway home it dawned on Holly that she'd forgotten all about telling Graham his raffle ticket had been drawn last night at the fund-raiser. There'd been so little opportunity for them to carry on adult conversation, and other topics had claimed priority.

He hadn't jogged her memory by asking, "What did you want to tell me in person?" Was he just not curious? Had he not gotten around to asking? Or had he simply assumed she'd come up with some flimsy pretext for seeing him?

"Answer C," Holly said, grimacing.

Braking for a red light, she dug into her handbag for her cell phone, then dropped it back in. If she phoned him now, she might wake the twins from their nap.

Do yourself a favor. Send him a fax at his office on Monday.

Holly knew she wouldn't take that advice from

herself. For one thing, she needed to find out whether or not he planned to make use of his prize and assign her a weeklong decorating project. If so, she would have to schedule the time.

The chances were practically nil that he would avail himself of her expertise. She expected a courteous brush-off from him. Still, she'd promised Ann to notify Graham, and notify him Holly would.

At home she played her phone messages and returned calls to clients and friends. Several people extended casual invitations. In truth, Holly wasn't in much of a mood for socializing that evening, but she wasn't about to sit around and mope, so she agreed to see a movie with a decorator friend, Patricia Connors, whose husband was out of town. They decided on the seven o'clock showing.

The movie, a romantic comedy, turned out to be as good as advertised. Afterward, her spirits much improved, Holly joined Patricia at a restaurant near the theater for a light supper. The two women relived particularly humorous parts of the movie as they ate. After splitting the bill, they said goodnight.

It was only ten o'clock, not too late to call Graham, Holly decided as she let herself into her house. He wasn't likely to be entertaining female company tonight. And by now surely the twins would be asleep.

Holly used the phone in her office, emphasizing to herself that the call was *strictly* business.

Graham answered between the first and second ring. "Hello."

He sounded bone weary and the timbre of his voice made her wonder if he was lying down.

"Hi, this is Holly. I hope I didn't wake you up." She stiffened her posture when he didn't reply immediately, evidently needing a second to adjust to her identity.

"No, I hadn't gone to sleep yet."

"But you had gone to bed. I'm sorry. I'll call at a more convenient time."

"Right now I don't have a bed of my own," he said, ignoring her final remark. "I'm bunking on the sofa these days." She could hear a muffled yawn.

"You gave the twins your bedroom?"

"It was either that or a pallet on the floor."

"I thought those condos had two bedrooms."

"They do. But I use the smaller one as a study. I have bookcases in there. A computer."

"So you'll sacrifice your study and turn that room over to the twins." Common sense said he didn't plan to sleep indefinitely on the sofa.

"Do you think that's okay at their age for them to share a bedroom? God, I hate to think of moving somewhere else right now."

"Sure, I think it's okay as a temporary arrangement. You can do something really cute with creating two separate spaces, a girl space and a boy space.''

"It's not a large room we're talking about."

"There's a closet for clothes, right? All you'll require in the way of furniture is a single bed and a chest of drawers for each twin. Preferably not matching. Two separate sections of wall shelves will do nicely for their toys. Maybe murals on opposite walls.'' Holly's enthusiasm warmed her voice.

"Murals?" he repeated doubtfully.

"Yes. A cowboy or sports motif on Justin's side and something more feminine, say a ballerina or a scene out of Snow White on Jennifer's side. Don't you like the idea?''

"Of course. It's a neat idea, but I'll be doing good to get the room cleared out and furniture bought in the next couple of weeks, let alone hire an artist to paint murals.''

What better opening for Holly to tell him the purpose of her call? "You're in luck,'' she declared lightly. "Last night at our drawing you won the Decorating Consultant for a Week prize. I'm the decorator whose services you get free, and it so happens I minored in fine art in college.''

"You're joking."

She didn't pretend to misunderstand his amazement. "No, I don't joke about working free of charge."

"This is all on the up-and-up? I mean, my raffle ticket was drawn…?"

He didn't finish his sentence, perhaps reacting to Holly's sharply drawn breath.

"Are you suggesting that I rigged our drawing?" she demanded, incredulous as well as insulted.

His silence was proof that he had indeed considered that possibility. "It just struck me as something of a coincidence," he said lamely.

"Exactly the sort of trick Heather would pull, right?"

His sigh came over the line. "Holly, don't take offense. Please."

He hadn't denied that he was judging her by Heather's behavior.

"Ann Johnson asked me to contact you, and now I have," she said crisply. "I'll need to know whether you'll want to take advantage of my services."

"God knows I could use your help right now."

"Yes, you need my help. And you'll utilize my skills if you put the welfare of the twins first. They can have a special room of their own instead of just a makeshift bedroom. But you make up your own mind and let me know what you've decided." Holly cut the connection.

The bullheaded so-and-so would probably communicate with her through his secretary to say, "Thanks, but no thanks." Which was just fine with Holly.

Not true.

Holly wanted to create the delightful room she'd begun to envision for Justin and Jennifer. During those few hours today, she'd already grown fond of both children. It was impossible not to feel concerned about them and wish she could play some role in brightening their young lives.

Despite her irritation at Graham, it was impossible not to be concerned about him, too.

Graham listened to the buzz of the dead line a few seconds before he pressed the disconnect button on his portable phone.

Holly's righteous indignation had rung true. The raffle drawing had undoubtedly been on the up and up. He felt foolish for having reacted suspiciously. It had just come as such a surprise to learn he'd won Holly's services.

She hadn't exactly chased him, but she'd made it plain she was interested in dating him. He'd learned his lesson with Heather and had shied away from women who came on to him. Hell, he'd shied away from women period the past four plus years since his affair with Heather had ended so abruptly with her dumping him. Of course, now he understood her underlying motives.

Comprehension didn't make him any less confident of himself in sizing up the opposite sex. Quite the opposite. He'd learned he was even a bigger fool than he'd believed. Who was to say he'd be smarter in future relationships?

Graham was ready to admit he was probably being unfair to Holly, not giving her a chance to prove she wasn't like Heather in personality and character, but he didn't have the time or energy to put into dating anyway. He had all he could handle coping with sudden parenthood.

So what was he going to do about Holly? Should he turn over to her the headache of fixing up a bedroom for the twins?

Should and would, Graham decided. He'd give her a key to his condo and a ballpark budget and say, "Do it."

There shouldn't be any need for consultations. She would have a free hand. She could come during the day while he was at work. Call him a coward, but he didn't trust himself to be around her and keep his guard up. He was too attracted to her, too tempted to be friends.

Graham closed his eyes and let himself visualize Holly as she'd looked that morning standing outside his door in her jeans and T-shirt. Honey-blond hair tucked behind her ears in a casual style. A warm smile on her lips and her pretty blue eyes alight with humor and intelligence. Definitely a nice sight that had stirred pleasure in him even in his unhappy state of mind.

As tired as he was tonight, lying there in the darkness of his living room wearing nothing but his underwear, it would be easy to fantasize about Holly and get himself turned on sexually. Easy, but totally stupid. Graham sat up abruptly, dropping the cordless phone in the process.

He snapped on a lamp and searched for the TV remote, finally locating it under a chair cushion. After thirty minutes of mindless channel surfing, he glanced at his watch and decided he should go ahead and call Holly tonight. He figured she would appreciate finding out this weekend that she needed to schedule in time for turning his study into a bedroom for the twins.

Graham delayed long enough to drag on his jeans before he looked up Holly's home number. It was silly, but he felt too vulnerable talking to her in a near-naked state.

She answered and sounded awake but extremely relaxed.

"Hi, it's Graham," he said. "I took the chance you might still be up."

"No problem. Did you make up your mind?"

"Yes, it was pretty much a no-brainer. I called to give you the go-ahead on the bedroom project." Did he hear water splashing?

"Fine."

Now gurgling sounds.

"Whoops! I almost slipped," she gasped.

"What are you doing?"

"Getting out of the bathtub. I took a long, hot soak."

Thanks for sharing that with me, Graham thought dryly, captivated by an X-rated vision of a nude Holly, all wet and rosy-skinned and smelling of sweetly scented soap.

"Why don't I call you back in a few minutes?" he suggested.

"Just hold on a second while I wrap myself in a towel. Okay," she said after several seconds. "What are your plans for tomorrow?"

He was too taken aback to reply immediately. "If I work up the courage, I might venture out to the supermarket with the twins and buy their kind of cereal and some cookies. Other than that, I'm playing tomorrow by ear. Why?"

"I'd like to come by and see the room. The sooner I get started, the sooner I'll be finished and out of your hair."

"Sure, you can come by," he said, none too happy over the leap of his pulse at the prospect of seeing her tomorrow. "What's best for you, morning or afternoon?"

"Morning. Is nine or nine-thirty too early?"

"Unless the twins sleep later than they did today, seven o'clock wouldn't be too early."

"What kind of cereal do they like? I could stop by the supermarket on the way," she stated in a matter-of-fact tone.

"That would be great, if it's not too much trouble," he said gratefully.

"If it were too much trouble, I wouldn't have offered. And I was thinking of Jennifer and Justin, not you."

Graham clamped his jaws to keep from saying anything conciliatory. It was far better for her to stay annoyed at him. Let her keep him at arm's length instead of vice versa. "They each like a different cereal. Fortunately, not the sugar-coated stuff." He named the cereals.

She repeated the names, as though making a mental list. "Anything else? Juice?"

"I have orange juice and apple juice. That'll stave off their hunger until you get here. I should warn you in advance. They'll be overjoyed to see you again. This afternoon they were almost inconsolable when they woke up from their nap and you'd gone."

"Poor darlings. They're probably confused about people suddenly disappearing from their lives." Her voice was warm with sympathy and affection.

"You're good with kids," he commented.

"I love children," she said simply. "My favorite part of decorating clients' homes is doing their children's rooms and nurseries. Whenever possible, I like to get acquainted with the little girls and boys in order to create a space that's perfect for them. Tomorrow I'll try to get some hints about Jennifer's and Justin's preferences in colors and storybook characters and so forth.''

Graham listened to her note of sincerity and remembered the words she'd spoken at the park today, refuting any similarity in character between herself and Heather. *But I am* not *devious and manipulative.*

Holly seemed to be honest and straightforward, but so had Heather. He hadn't once suspected that Heather was devious and manipulative, even after she broke off with him so suddenly.

For all he knew, he was being taken in again.

Chapter Four

"Thank God, you're here," Graham said fervently, swinging the door wide open. "I made the mistake of telling the twins you were coming over."

Today he was wearing jeans again and a different T-shirt. His dark brown hair was rumpled and he looked more haggard than he had yesterday. But no less masculine and appealing. Holly could feel her annoyance at him melting into sympathy.

Jennifer and Justin brushed past his legs. Clapping their hands and jumping up and down, they chanted excitedly, "Oh, boy, Holly's here! Oh, boy, Holly's here!"

"What a nice reception!" she exclaimed. After first handing Graham the grocery bags she held, she knelt and encircled both twins, giving them a hug. Two pairs of little arms hugged her around the neck. Warm, sweet emotion welled up in Holly's chest.

"Can we go to that same playground again?" Jennifer asked hopefully.

"Can we?" Justin begged.

"Holly can't stay a long time," Graham spoke up, indirectly telling them no. "Remember, I told you she has important things to do."

Nothing seemed more important to Holly at the moment than spending a few hours with these two darling children—and their father, despite the fact he didn't want her around.

"Why don't we go and fix you both some breakfast?" she suggested, rising. The best tactic would be to evade the whole issue of going to the playground. "Your daddy asked me to buy your favorite cereal. Wasn't that nice of him?"

"Will you fix mine?" Jennifer implored.

Graham opened his mouth and closed it when Holly silenced him with a telling look that said, "Could I answer for myself, please?"

"Unless your daddy objects, I'll fix yours and Justin's." She addressed Graham. "Would you like to take a long walk or go for a run? You look like you could use some exercise."

From his expression she might have been a prison warden offering an inmate a furlough out into the world. "I'd love to go for a run. If you're sure you don't mind. I was up at five, but I couldn't leave the kids alone."

"Take as long as you want. It will give me a chance to ask Jennifer and Justin some questions and get some ideas about decorating their room. Come along, kids."

Graham didn't need more urging. He bounded up the stairs while she ushered the twins into the kitchen.

In five minutes he reappeared in running attire. Holly glanced up from pouring milk into bowls of cereal. Her quick once-over made her pulse hum. In his skimpy nylon shorts, Graham definitely qualified as a hunk.

"Feel free to go upstairs and take your room measurements or whatever," he said.

"Is the study locked?"

"Yes. But here's a set of house keys for you." He reached to a decorative brass key rack on the wall, held up a key ring and then hung it back in place.

"Have a good run."

"Thanks. I owe you."

Holly treated herself to another once-over as he departed. The rear view left nothing to be desired, either. Hard-muscled calves and thighs. Nice rear end. Lean, powerful upper torso.

Darn it, she liked his looks. She liked *him.*

And she bet he would like her, if he gave himself half a chance. But he was bound and determined not to like her because she reminded him of Heather Booth.

"I don't want sliced bananas on my cereal, but Justin does." Jennifer's reminder brought Holly back to the present.

She served the children, joining them at the table while they ate hungrily. Noting that they were crouched on their knees in their chairs, she made a mental note to call to Graham's attention the need for booster seats.

"That's a pretty pink blouse you're wearing, Jennifer," Holly complimented.

"She likes pink," Justin said. "Lots of her clothes are pink, but not mine."

"Little boys don't wear pink," Jennifer explained. "It's a girl color."

Holly couldn't resist broadening the young minds already narrowed by society's gender-specific rules. "Actually, there are no girl colors and boy colors. I remember seeing your daddy wearing a pink-striped shirt that looked very nice on him with his dark brown hair and eyes." How easy it was to conjure up an attractive picture even though the memory was a year old.

"And my daddy's not a sissy, is he?" responded Justin.

"No, he's very masculine."

While Holly was formulating a gentle lecture on classifying any male as a "sissy," Jennifer directed the subject away from their father, stating, "Justin likes blue the best. Don't you, Justin?"

By the time the twins had finished their breakfast, they'd revealed a world of information about their tastes and interests. After the kitchen was tidy again, Holly took them upstairs with her to inspect the room that would be theirs. She also stuck her head inside the door of the larger master bedroom.

Justin and Jennifer chattered nonstop and competed with each other for her attention. Several times Holly had to play referee when they began bickering and even exchanged blows. But they were easily distracted at their age and also eager to please. Holly thoroughly enjoyed their company and found herself thinking, This is such fun. I'm almost certain I would love raising a child and could juggle career and motherhood.

Being *almost certain* wasn't good enough, which was one reason Holly hadn't reached any firm decision yet about having a baby or adopting. Evidently Heather Booth had wanted very badly to be a mother and had believed she could successfully juggle career and single parenthood. But had she achieved a balance? Justin and Jennifer mentioned their nanny, Mary, far more often than they mentioned Mommy, raising a question about how much time their mommy had devoted to them.

I'm not Heather, Holly told herself. I'm me, despite what Graham thinks.

Graham ran along Monroe to Carondelet Street, hooked a right and continued to the lakefront. Branches of tall trees on either side turned the street into a cool tunnel dappled by sunlight. God, it felt great to take long strides, his lungs sucking in morning air. He welcomed the euphoria that flushed away fatigue and relieved some of the mental strain of the past three days.

For the first time in his life, Graham found himself confronted with circumstances he might not be able to handle. ''I can do this,'' he'd said aloud and silently over and over, not believing his own pep talk.

He didn't have any choice. He *had* to deal with being a father because he *was* one without wanting to be. It was a role forced upon him not just for a year or two or even ten years, but *from now on, for the rest of his life*.

The reality put Graham in a cold sweat. This is a nightmare, he found himself thinking time and time again.

But he wasn't so self-centered that he worried

only about himself and his happiness. He worried about Jennifer and Justin, too, and felt terrible on their behalf. They deserved a father who doted on them, who carried around photos and showed them proudly to other people.

Last night—and the night before—after they'd gone to sleep, Graham had tiptoed upstairs every hour or so to check on them and relieve his anxiety. They'd looked innocent and vulnerable in slumber. He'd felt a whole mix of emotions. Relief that they were safe and at rest and that he was off duty for a few hours. Dread at the thought of morning when they would wake up and another day would begin. Guilt because gazing at them filled him with acute concern for their welfare, but not fatherly affection.

Maybe if he could get the hang of a day-to-day routine and start feeling more up to the challenge of single parenthood, bonding would occur, Graham reflected as he ran along the lakefront. Intellectually he accepted the fact that the twins were *his* children, but there was no gut message that said *my kids*.

His lukewarm attitude toward fatherhood might have been a clue all along that he wasn't suited to be a parent. If so, that meant he just had to work that much harder to overcome his deficiencies.

Graham's route took him to the far end of Lakeshore Drive where he looped around and headed back along the mile-and-a-half stretch of lakefront.

Instead of veering right when he reached Carondelet, he continued to the next street but resisted the strong urge to prolong his run. He didn't want to take advantage of Holly.

It had been very kind of her to give him a badly needed break. She seemed like such a considerate, kind person. If only he could trust her—

You can't, Graham told himself, not continuing that dangerous line of thought. He couldn't afford to let down his guard with Holly for one second. She was too much like Heather in too many ways to discount the similarities. Earlier, when he'd come downstairs after changing into his running shorts, Holly had checked him out just like Heather always had, though not quite so blatantly.

And he'd reacted like a dumb, susceptible male, with the twins right there as warning flags. What was *wrong* with him that he fell for the type of woman who saw a man she wanted and went after him?

"Dumb, dumb, dumb," Graham muttered with self-contempt, slowing to a walk to cool down when he was a quarter of a mile from his condo complex. He felt a hundred percent better physically. A shower would leave him even more energized.

Entering his condo, he could hear Justin and Jennifer arguing in the living room. Their raised voices brought reality crashing down on him again.

"I want to go first!"

"You always get to go first!"

"I'm a girl, and girls get to go first!"

"That's not fair!"

Holly intervened, her tone calm and unruffled. Graham's tension eased. "Justin's right," she was saying. "It wouldn't be fair for girls to always play first in any game. How would you feel in his place, Jennifer?"

There was no answer. Graham could easily imagine his little daughter, lips pursed stubbornly and arms folded across her chest.

"Let her be first," Justin said disgustedly.

"No, you mustn't always give in to Jennifer. It's not good for her. She has to learn to take turns with girls and boys."

"Okay. Justin, you can go first." Jennifer relented in a sulky voice.

Graham made his entrance, feeling cowardly that he'd waited out of sight until Holly settled the controversy.

The three of them sat around a pink board game on the living room carpet. Something to do with ladders, he vaguely noted.

"Hi," Holly greeted him with a smile. "Did you have a good run?"

"A great run. Could I impose on you another ten minutes while I grab a quick shower?"

"No problem."

"After you have your shower, you could play, too," said Justin shyly.

"He's too big. There isn't room for him to sit down by us," Jennifer stated, quick to nix the idea of his joining them.

"Yes, there is." Justin scooted over, creating a space between him and Holly.

She met Graham's gaze and he sensed he was on trial somehow.

"Sure, I'll play," he said. "But somebody will have to explain the rules."

"It's easy," Justin assured him. "We'll tell you what to do."

When Graham came downstairs after his shower, Holly and the children had taken a break, delaying starting the game. They resumed their same positions.

"Why don't you sit between Justin and Jennifer?" Holly suggested before he could lower himself to the floor beside her.

Justin obediently moved over. Graham hesitated, expecting some objection from his daughter. When there was none, he followed Holly's direction.

"First Justin. Then me. Then Holly. Then you," Jennifer stated.

"Good idea for me to go last," Graham said, half-amused by her stubborn refusal to make friends with him. His sense of humor had been rejuvenated along with the rest of him. "It'll give me a chance to get the hang of the game."

While Justin was proceeding as the first player, Graham took the opportunity to tug his jeans higher on his thighs, freeing up more room for him to sit in a cross-legged position. He happened to look over at Holly and caught her watching him make himself more comfortable. Graham frowned, not pleased with his body's reaction to her interest. She lifted her shoulders in a tiny shrug of apology. *So I'm human. Don't make a big deal out of nothing,* she telegraphed in quick defense of herself.

"Is that how many spaces I go, Holly?" Justin asked.

"Hmm. Let's count to double-check."

Graham set his jaw and focused his attention on the simple game. It took two for sexual byplay, and that was a game he *wasn't* playing.

"Aren't they sweet?" Holly said softly. "They look so angelic asleep, don't they?"

Graham expelled a breath. "Thank God for naps." He kept his voice low, too. "It's such a relief when they conk out, except for the knowledge that they're just refueling all that energy."

He and Holly stood behind his living room sofa gazing at the twins, who'd just fallen asleep at opposite ends of the sofa following lunch. Seconds earlier they'd been kicking each other and bickering.

"These two can keep you on your toes," she admitted, "but they're not holy terrors, like some children I've been around. Don't you feel lucky that they're both so bright and active?"

"I'd be lying if I claimed to feel lucky about the developments of the last three days," he said soberly. "Nor do I consider these two in the least 'lucky' to draw me as a parent."

Holly sighed and made a movement to reach out and touch him. She checked herself and folded her arms tightly across her midriff. "Give yourself some time to adjust. A year from now you may look back and realize that being a father is the greatest thing that ever happened to you."

"For their sake, I hope so. They're stuck with me."

"Personally, I think Jennifer and Justin could have done a whole lot worse than drawing you for a parent. I daresay the majority of men wouldn't handle this same situation as conscientiously as you're doing."

He shrugged off her compliment. "I'll put on some coffee if you're staying."

"You let me promise them I would be here when they woke up from their nap," she reminded him. "Short of an emergency, I'm not going to break my word. But don't bother with the coffee. Let's go upstairs and—'' She broke off when Graham backed away a half step. Hands on hips, she eyed him indignantly. ''Would you get your mind out of the gutter? Earlier today I came up with an idea that would eliminate doing away with your study altogether and I wanted to explain it to you.''

''Oh. Okay.'' Graham was still reluctant about going upstairs with her.

''For your information, I'm *not* desperate to get you into bed,'' she informed him. ''I happen to prefer a willing sex partner.''

''That won't ever be me,'' Graham stated as forcefully as he could, considering the damn conversation was turning him on.

''Fine. I'll live. Are you interested in my idea or not?''

''Yes, I'm interested.'' He gestured toward the stairs.

Her jeans molding her shapely rear end, she marched in front of him, muttering irritably, ''Of all the men on the North Shore, I don't know *why* I had to find you the most attractive.''

Graham formed replies and swallowed them, deciding against saying anything.

Upstairs she led him first into the smaller bedroom, where she'd left her tape measure and a writing tablet. Briskly businesslike, she measured the bookcase units and the computer desk, reeling off dimensions already jotted down on the tablet. Graham sensed that she was buying time and cooling off.

"My idea is to turn the master bedroom into a combination bedroom and study," she said, snapping the release on the metal tape measure and letting it retract noisily. "There's room enough if the furniture were rearranged."

"Hmm. I like that plan," Graham said.

"Do we dare go in there so I can show you? Or would you rather I draw you a sketch?" She flipped over to a clean page on the tablet, her movements expressing simmering annoyance.

"You don't have to be sarcastic." He led the way into his bedroom.

"The bed could go over here." She pointed. "The chest of drawers there. And the armchair and floor lamp in that corner."

Graham was nodding, quickly grasping her room layout. "That leaves the area over there free for bookcases and computer desk and filing cabinet. It'll be a little crowded, but it'll work well."

Holly looked slightly mollified. "Well, why don't we get started?"

"Now?"

"What else is there to do? We have some time to kill while the twins are asleep."

So help him, Graham couldn't keep from glancing at the bed with regret. "I don't expect you to do manual labor as a part of your bargain,'' he protested.

"It's up to you," she said. "Do you want to rearrange the furniture, or not?"

She was right. They had an hour or more to spend together. Better to keep busy, Graham conceded. "You supervise," he told her.

She stood back and watched for a few seconds, but soon ended up helping. By the time he'd maneuvered the bed across the carpet, employing pushing and pulling techniques, she'd already removed the drawers from the dresser and stacked them to one side and unplugged the lamps.

"Like so?" he inquired.

"A couple of feet more to the right."

Next he moved the dresser. When it was in place to her satisfaction, she began helping him replace the drawers, not heeding Graham's statement, "I'll get those."

They were passing each other, with him giving her a wide berth, when he caught his foot in the cord of the floor lamp. Graham was carrying a drawer and she was on her way to get another one.

"Be careful!" Holly exclaimed, leaping in front of him with arms outstretched to catch the lamp before it crashed to the floor. Graham hastily freed his hands, pitching the drawer with a sideways motion and at the same time trying to skid to a dead stop. But he bumped into her hard. She went down, her legs tangling with his and tripping him in the process. He fell half on top of her.

"Are you all right?" he asked in concern.

Her eyes were closed and she lay perfectly still.

"Holly, say something."

"Don't sound so alarmed. I'm okay," she mumbled weakly and rolled her head away from him. "Most of the breath got knocked out of me, falling flat on my back like this."

Graham gently framed her cheek and applied enough force to turn her head so that he could see her face. "Are you in pain? Did you break anything?"

"No, I'm fine. Honest." The protestation was none too strong.

"Why don't you open your eyes?"

"Because this feels nicer than it should, lying here...." Her eyelashes lifted, revealing her pretty blue eyes. With sudden insight, Graham knew the expression in them would be the same if he were about to make love to her.

Graham's breath caught in his throat and his heart began to thud in his chest. He was suddenly aware of her silken skin under his palm, aware that his body was still half covering hers. And *nice* wasn't really the word to describe the intense pleasure of their physical proximity.

"Don't look at me like that," he said, trying to frown.

''Just following orders.''

His gaze dropped to her mouth. Get up. Don't kiss her, he ordered himself while he was slowly bridging the distance between them, succumbing to temptation more powerful than the dictates of judgment.

Holly whispered his name and her hands clasped his head as their lips met. For a few seconds, Graham savored the sensuality of their new intimacy. But almost immediately the kiss turned passionate, with his tongue coupling urgently with hers. His hands took on a life of their own and were all over her, touching her breasts, her hips, her thighs.

Graham just couldn't seem to heed the voice of reason that said *Stop! Don't take this any further!*

Holly grabbed his hand before he could slide it between her thighs and take them both a step closer toward making love right there on the floor.

''Graham, stop a minute and cool off!'' she gasped.

''I'm too turned on to stop.'' He guided her hand to let her feel for herself the hard, swollen proof of his arousal.

''We would both be sorry afterward,'' she said with a note of regret.

Graham sucked in a deep breath and rolled away from her to sit up. ''It's a good thing one of us has some self-control.'' He sounded more resentful and frustrated than grateful, which was just the way he felt.

Holly sat up, too, hugging her legs. "Was it like that with you and Heather?" she asked hesitantly.

"Like what?"

"You know... Hot and hungry."

"Yes. While it lasted," he added.

"It's not surprising that you got her pregnant with twins."

Graham welcomed the bitter reminder of his affair with Heather. He was flooded with self-disgust at his behavior. "You would think I'd learn my lesson and wouldn't touch another woman without proper precautions."

"The fact that I remind you so much of her probably explains why you got so carried away."

"Any excuse is better than none, I guess." Graham stood up and retrieved the drawer he'd dropped.

She sat on the floor a moment longer before she rose to her feet, too, and righted the fallen lamp. "I'll go start emptying the bookshelves."

"Why don't you go downstairs and relax? Read a magazine?"

Without a word, she did his bidding and left the room.

Good. No collisions, Graham thought to himself, finishing the job alone.

Chapter Five

Holly escaped downstairs. She badly needed some time by herself to recover from that passionate escapade on the floor. How ironic that Graham was so intent on keeping up his defenses against her. The tables had turned.

Now *she* felt like the vulnerable party of the two.

Her lips were bruised from Graham's kisses. Her tongue still tasted his. Her breasts tingled from his caresses, the nipples hard and needy. Her lower body ached with sexual frustration. But it was the ache in her heart that worried her. The sense of rejection that came from knowing Graham hadn't been on the verge of making love to *her,* Holly

Beaumont, was much too deep. It hurt far more than she would have expected to be a Heather substitute.

Graham had obviously been crazy about the twins' mother. By his own admission, he'd proposed marriage to her. For all his bitterness, he wasn't over Heather.

No, thank you, I'm not acting as her stand-in. No matter how much I like him, she decided.

Holly stopped in the living room and stood for a few moments, gazing at the sleeping twins. The caring emotion that welled up seemed to intensify her inner turmoil.

Right now these precious children needed her as a stabilizing influence, at least temporarily while they made the adjustment from one home environment to another. Instinctively they trusted her and depended on her. Just because being around their father was problematic for Holly, could she desert them, becoming one more adult in their lives who had come and gone?

No, indeed.

Her conscience wouldn't allow her to do that.

In the kitchen Holly brewed coffee and settled at the table with her tablet. Forty-five minutes later when Graham came downstairs, she'd filled several pages and organized the week ahead to streamline the process of transforming his former study into a delightful bedroom for the twins. She'd also formulated ground rules for all further dealings with the twins' daddy.

"You mind if I join you?" Graham asked, pouring himself a mug of coffee.

"Please do." Holly gestured at the chair across from her.

He sat down, his manner anything but relaxed. "The study's all yours now."

"You got everything moved, even the books?"

"I just crammed them onto shelves. I figure I can arrange them later at my leisure once I reclaim my bedroom."

"That was fast work."

"Well, I wanted to get finished before Justin and Jennifer woke up." He took a gulp of coffee. "About what happened between us—"

"It won't happen again," Holly interrupted him in a firm voice. She flipped backward to a page in the tablet and tapped with her index finger. "See right here what I've written? Ground Rules. Number one. In the future treat Graham as an acquaintance and a client. Number two. Maintain a friendly, but strictly businesslike relationship." Key words were underlined twice.

Graham leaned over to stare down at the tablet. "You actually wrote all that down." He sounded slightly intrigued as well as amazed.

"I make a practice of writing things down. Instructions. Goals. As well as Things to Do lists."

He shifted sideways in his chair, a puzzled frown cutting lines between his eyebrows. "Why the sudden change in attitude? You were open to more than a 'friendly, but businesslike relationship' before. Weren't you?"

Holly nodded an affirmative. "But now I'm not. My reasons don't really matter. They're no negative reflection on you," she was quick to add. "I still find you very attractive, and I consider you a person of high moral character, but I've decided you're right in ruling out any kind of involvement between us. Enough said?"

Graham downed another big swallow of coffee. "This sudden turnabout must have something to do with what happened upstairs."

Apparently he didn't agree that enough had been said.

Holly shrugged. "It does."

"You certainly seemed responsive enough. Otherwise I'm sure I would have stopped right away. I don't force myself on women."

"Responsive? What happened was straight out of a romance novel. I went up in flames. Poof!" She gestured dramatically. "I wanted to tear your clothes off and let you tear my clothes off. I was wild to make love to you right there on the carpet. But you wouldn't have been making love to *me*. Which bothered me a whole lot."

"What do you mean—I wouldn't be making love to *you?*"

"Do I have to draw you a picture?" She rolled her eyes in exasperation. "Look, I've gotten a few wolf whistles in my time and even a marriage proposal or two, but no man has ever gotten *that* instantly turned on before by a first kiss."

Comprehension finally struck him. "You think I was imagining you were Heather."

"Correct. You get an A−. It was a timed quiz." The flippancy was for her own protection.

"I *wasn't* fantasizing about her," Graham said. "But I agree there's something bizarre about the fact that I haven't felt the same chemistry with anyone before or after Heather. Until now."

"Well, I'm not into bizarre anything. I'm pretty much your old-fashioned liberated woman." Holly suggested with her tone that they'd covered the subject sufficiently. She turned to a clean page and began sketching, conscious that he was watching her.

"You figure attraction can be turned off like a faucet?" he asked.

"I'm hopeful it can be talked to death."

Holly sensed her remark might have made him smile with wry amusement. She kept her gaze fixed on her pencil strokes, not daring to look at him.

A sound signaled they weren't alone anymore. Justin stood in the kitchen doorway, rubbing his eyes and yawning. His sister came up beside him, rubbing her eyes and yawning, too.

"Hey, sleepyheads," Holly greeted them affectionately, pushing back her chair.

Jennifer walked over and climbed up into her lap. Holly hugged the little girl and kissed her. Meanwhile Justin had moved closer, too. The expression on his small face was wistful.

"You can sit on your daddy's lap," Holly prompted.

The little boy looked questioningly at Graham, who was slow to respond but eventually gave his thigh an awkward pat. Justin walked over and Graham lifted him up.

Hug him, Holly urged silently. But her message went unheeded. Instead, Graham patted him gently on the back.

One step at a time, she thought.

"You said we could have cookies and milk after our nap, Holly," Jennifer reminded.

"Can we?" Justin directed the question shyly to his father.

Holly couldn't hold her tongue on the name issue any longer. At this rate, Graham's children would be half-grown before he encouraged them to address him as Daddy. "It's okay, Justin, for you to call your father Daddy."

Disappointingly, Graham said nothing, letting silence serve as acquiescence. His small son immediately acted on her permission, his voice still endearingly shy. "Can we have milk and cookies, Daddy?"

Jennifer announced with a note of belligerence, "I'm not calling him Daddy."

"You both can have milk and cookies," Graham said, standing up and transferring Justin into the chair.

Holly smothered a sigh. She wished Graham had made some response to Jennifer, but Rome hadn't been built in a day.

"I'll help you clean up before I go," Holly offered.

"No, I'd rather deal with the mess tomorrow morning before they wake up. I should have the energy then and you've done more than enough. Thanks again for helping me get the kids into a good preschool on the spur of the moment."

"It was nothing. As I told you, the director is a former client."

"Well, I'm grateful. I was in a bind."

"I hope the arrangement works well for the twins and for you. Now, since you have everything under control, I'll say good-night."

Don't invite her to stay, Graham ordered himself. What the hell. He was too beat to be tempted tonight. Yet he didn't want to be alone. "I have a good Merlot I'm going to uncork. Would you like a glass?''

She hesitated briefly before accepting.

"Push some toys out of your way and make yourself comfortable," he said. "I'll be right back."

The wine was in the kitchen and as Graham entered and glanced at the table, he winced. Jennifer had gotten hold of a ballpoint pen during the afternoon and scrawled on the wooden surface, penetrating the finish in places where she'd pressed down hard. Also visible were greasy child-size hand imprints that a hasty wiping after supper hadn't removed. The ceramic tile floor around the table was strewn with bits of food. Graham recognized cookie crumbs and clumps of cheese-coated macaroni.

He didn't consider himself finicky by any means, but he was used to reasonably clean, orderly conditions at home. Without a full-time maid, he guessed he'd better relax his standards. Relax them a whole lot.

Shaking his head over that conclusion, Graham selected a bottle of wine.

When he rejoined Holly, carrying the open bottle and two stemmed glasses, she was curled up at one end of the sofa. Graham set the glasses on the coffee table, poured wine and handed her a glass before he went and put a CD on the stereo, stepping over toys strewn on the carpet. With soothing music playing, he settled on the opposite end of the sofa and sipped his wine. Closing his eyes, he drew in a deep breath and expelled it. The tension in his body eased slightly.

"Day three of fatherhood. Thanks to you, I survived it and so did the twins," he said. "You very kindly sacrificed your whole Sunday."

She'd even stuck around to help with the ordeal of giving the twins their baths, getting them into pajamas and putting them to bed.

"It wasn't a sacrifice," she replied. "I had fun with Jennifer and Justin. You will, too, once you relax a little and let yourself enjoy them."

"I hope you're right." Graham wasn't optimistic.

"Don't be afraid to show them affection. Justin will respond now, and you can win Jennifer over in a matter of time."

"How can I show them fatherly affection without feeling it? Because I don't," he admitted soberly. "What I feel is a heavy burden of responsibility. Which means, I suppose, there's something lacking in me."

"No, there isn't anything lacking in you. Remember that married couples usually have nine months to prepare themselves for being parents. This has all been a terrible shock."

"I'll say."

He refilled her wineglass and his and settled back

again, considerably closer than before. The wine and music combined with her presence were doing wonders for his morale. "Do you like the Merlot?"

"It's fabulous. Smooth and mellow. I'll have to memorize the label."

"Tell you what. I'll buy a case and make you a present of it." Graham slid lower and rested his head against the sofa cushion, closing his eyes. "Damn, this is nice."

She didn't answer, but the silence was companionable. Graham savored the flavor of the wine on his tongue and mentally hummed along with the music. *I'd better open my eyes before I fall asleep,* he thought.

The self-warning came too late. Drowsiness had suddenly turned his eyelids to lead.

Holly bent forward and gently rescued Graham's wineglass. At close range, she paused a moment to admire his hands. Even lax, they were manly and strong and yet well shaped. Hands suited to wielding an architect's pencil skillfully. Hands suited to caressing a woman's body...

Remember your ground rules, dearie, Holly reminded herself, setting his glass on the table. The sensible thing for her to do was to ease up without disturbing him and go home, but it seemed a shame not to finish her glass of wine. And what was the danger of staying a while longer, with Graham sound asleep?

None.

Holly sighed, studying him with pleasure. Rumpled brown hair, clean-cut features, strong jawline, sexy mouth. Snore, she instructed him silently. Drool. Do something to turn me off.

Poor guy was having such a rough time, assuming the role of single dad to two active three-and-a-half-year-olds. It was impossible not to feel sympathy for him, especially since he was so hard on himself. Not once during the weekend had he whined and complained to Holly, saying something like "Why did this happen to me?" Instead he took full responsibility for his actions as biological father. That kind of mind-set was tremendously appealing to Holly. His only question had been, "Why were these children unlucky enough to draw me?"

She hadn't detected any resentment on his part toward Jennifer and Justin. He hadn't spoken the first harsh word to them, not even to his daughter when she'd damaged the kitchen table. It had fallen to Holly to scold the little girl several times for her bratty behavior.

For the twins' sake and for his own survival, Graham needed to learn how to be a disciplinarian. He needed to learn a whole host of parenting skills.

Most of all he needed to develop confidence in his aptitude for being a good daddy.

Earlier that day Holly had accepted the fact that she couldn't abandon the twins. Well, she couldn't abandon Graham, either.

And those ground rules she'd formulated... They would have to be revised and expanded. In truth, when she'd written them down, she'd already blown any possibility of treating Graham strictly as a client. It was silly to pretend she could stop being attracted to him. She couldn't.

That didn't mean Holly was any less definite about the wisdom of keeping her relationship with Graham platonic. Sex was much too complicated, given her resemblance to Heather and given Graham's obvious need now for a wife and permanent mother for Justin and Jennifer.

Holly wasn't a candidate, regardless of how fond she'd become of all three of them.

"Good night, Friend," she whispered and kissed him on his brow. He made a sound and turned his face toward her, causing her heart to leap with panic. But his eyes remained closed and he remained deeply asleep.

Holly resisted a second tender kiss.

She set down her empty glass and tiptoed out.

"You've already lined up a painter, for today?" Graham sounded amazed.

"It's a small job, and I begged and groveled." Holly braked for a red light. She'd called Graham from her car phone. "My problem is unlocking your condo for him. I forgot to take the set of keys when I was leaving last night."

"I noticed this morning you hadn't taken them. Sorry about conking out on you like that." His embarrassment came over the line. "Hope I didn't snore."

"You should provide your guests with earplugs," she teased him. "Just kidding."

"I wish you'd woken me up."

"I didn't have the heart. You were sacked out so peacefully." Holly pushed the memory away, disturbed by her tender emotion. "But about the key. Shall I swing by your office? I'm only a few blocks away."

"I was on my way out of the office. Why don't I meet you at the condo?"

"Works for me." She kept a lilt of gladness out of her voice. But there was no denying she *was* glad she would see him today for a few minutes.

They arrived almost at the same time, he driving his pickup truck. He looked like the typical young professional man on the North Shore, dressed in khaki slacks and a shirt and tie. Typical except that he was more good-looking than average—in Holly's eyes, at least.

"Hi," she greeted him as they met on the walkway. "What good timing that you wore that pink shirt today. Yesterday I got into a discussion with Jennifer and Justin about gender-specific colors and I told them about seeing you wearing that very shirt." Great, Holly, she chastised herself, you just revealed the fact that you could describe anything in his wardrobe he's ever worn around you.

"I got a rehash of the discussion this morning. You didn't convince Jennifer, by the way."

"Jennifer's no pushover when it comes to changing her ideas."

"Especially her dislike of me."

"It could be that she hasn't been around men very much. She and Justin seem to have lived a very sheltered life with no male influences. They never mention any man friend of Heather's or even their grandfather."

"Heather obviously had a man friend since she met with her fatal accident when the two of them were away together, on vacation in Italy."

They'd reached the front door. Graham unlocked it and followed Holly inside.

"Who did she leave the twins with?" she asked. He'd told her the sketchy circumstances of Heather's tragic automobile accident at some point over the weekend, but the conversation, like so many others, had gotten interrupted.

"They stayed at Heather's house. The nanny came and took care of them in the daytime. A nighttime sitter spent the night. I gather it was a rather frequent arrangement.''

''I hate to be critical of someone who isn't around to defend herself, but frankly, Heather doesn't come across as having been an ideal mother.''

''Her aunt said quite bluntly that Heather wasn't a good mother. She apparently discovered the reality was different from the fantasy of single motherhood.''

''There are a lot of things people can find out by trial and error, but discovering whether they like being parents shouldn't be one of them.''

''I agree totally. Which is why I told Heather I was doubtful I would ever want kids. Little did I realize she was screening me as an applicant for sperm donor.'' His bitterness hadn't lessened, but it was laced with acceptance, as though he was getting more used to the idea of his ex-girlfriend's duplicity.

''Your outspokenness on the subject of fatherhood only served to salve her conscience, I suppose.''

''Apparently.''

They'd been moving toward the kitchen as they talked. Holly bit her lips, but indignant words burst out anyway. ''God, I can't believe you think I'm like her! I would *never* trick any man the way she tricked you.'' She pocketed the set of keys she'd forgotten last night. "When I meet a guy I'm interested in dating, I spell out my position on marriage. If you remember, I made sure you knew where I was coming from before I asked you to lunch while we were working on that project a year ago." He'd made an excuse and turned her down, leaving her in the dark about his real reason.

Graham's smile was cynical. "I do remember. Heather also warned me in advance that she was a career woman. That didn't keep me from falling for her. Tell me this. Have any of the men you dated gotten serious about you anyway?"

"Yes," Holly admitted.

"What did you do? Drop them like a hot potato?"

"Naturally, I broke off with them. For their sake."

"Right." He brushed past her and strode toward the door of the laundry room. "You're not so naive, Holly, that you really believe you can draw an imaginary line in man-woman relationships and post a sign, Don't Fall In Love With Me. Sorry, it doesn't work that way. Not with men. I speak from experience," he added over his shoulder, his tone grim.

"What the heck do you expect a woman who decides against marrying to do?" she demanded, following behind him. Even in her ruffled state, she noted that he had cleaned up this morning. "I like men. I enjoy masculine company. I think I have a lot to offer as a female companion.''

"That you do.''

So had Heather, Holly could guess he was recalling bitterly. Frustrated, she watched him measure laundry detergent into the washing machine and load it with small soiled garments. His actions reminded her of something she'd meant to call to his attention and had forgotten.

"I noticed last night when I was getting clean pajamas for Justin and Jennifer that they each had only a couple of outfits left to wear to preschool,'' she said. "Is their great-aunt sending along the rest of their clothes?''

"She promised to send more toys, but she said the nanny claimed to have packed all the clothing that fit them. They supposedly had a recent growth spurt and outgrew most of their clothes.'' He twisted the dial. "I checked labels for the sizes. I thought I'd call a couple of stores with children's departments at the North Shore mall and have the salesclerks pick out some outfits. I can squeeze in a quick trip over to Slidell one day and pay for them.''

"The stores stay open until 9:00 p.m.,'' Holly pointed out.

Graham gave her a horrified look. "No way am I taking those two into a mall by myself. I can just picture trying to hold on to their hands and carry packages at the same time."

She could picture the scene, too, and smiled with empathy. "They could give you the slip, all right. I'd be happy to go along any night this week. My evenings are free, for a change. You could shop with Justin while Jennifer and I hit the little girls' section."

"That's too big an imposition."

"I would love it. It would be loads of fun, picking out cute little girl clothes."

"You're sure you don't mind?"

"Positive."

He slumped with relief as though her offer had taken a load off his shoulders. "Pick whatever night is best for you."

Holly gestured, lifting both hands palm up as though to say she was entirely flexible. "Tonight?"

Graham was quick to agree, and they finalized plans. No sooner had he departed for a job site than the painter arrived. Greeting Rob Tauzin, Holly was conscious she was smiling far too radiantly.

Rob, a man in his mid-thirties, was one of the best and most reliable painters on the North Shore, in Holly's opinion. He was always her first choice on any decorating job. The fact that she threw so much work his way accounted for his presence here today. Plus, it was obvious that he liked her personally and respected her, too. In his offhanded way, he'd bestowed compliments in the past for her originality and talent in her profession.

"So where's this rush job?" Rob inquired, readjusting his baseball cap. He wore his long black hair in a ponytail.

"Follow me."

Holly led him upstairs.

While she was explaining the decorating concept for the twins' bedroom and giving Rob instructions, he nodded and several times made approving responses. Holly couldn't help noticing, though, that he was eyeing her quizzically.

"What do you think?" she asked after she'd finished her spiel.

"Neat idea. And no problem, from my end."

Holly waited for him to say more.

"These clients must be friends of yours," he guessed. "I mean, you're always hyped up about a new project you're tackling." But not *this* hyped up, his shrug implied.

"I've met the children and I fell in love with them," she admitted. "They're twins. They just lost their mother and have come to live with their dad."

He made a tsk-tsking sound of sympathy.

"You know him," Holly went on. "Graham Knight, the architect."

"Oh, yeah. Nice guy. Didn't realize he was ever married and had kids." Rob looked thoughtful, then suddenly became all business, and shifted his attention to the walls of the room. "Just one suggestion. How 'bout making the dividing line between the pink and blue sides wavy instead of straight?"

"I love it!" she exclaimed. "Rob, you're a genius!"

He grinned, lifting his baseball cap and settling it snugly again on his head. "I wouldn't go that far. Take me an hour, maybe an hour and a half, to slap on a coat of white primer. It'll dry fast, and you can draw that wavy line for me before I come back in the morning. Okeydokey?"

Holly was squinting at the walls, visualizing curving lines. "Don't worry. I won't hold you up," she promised absently.

Whistling a classic Beatles tune, Rob began unfolding a drop cloth to protect the carpet. Holly left him to his work. Downstairs, she remembered the load of clothes and went to the laundry room. The washing machine had finished its cycle. She transferred the clothes to the dryer and started them tumbling. It was little enough to do to help Graham out.

Even though she was making this job top priority, Holly had other decorating projects going that she needed to keep tabs on. One was in progress in a nearby subdivision where one of her clients was having wallpaper hung. She drove there and found everything going well. Next she stopped off at the shop of a seamstress and conferred with her about a big order of fancy pillows for still a different client. On her way back to Graham's place, she dropped off some fabric swatches at the home of a third client, a doctor's wife.

An hour and a half had passed when she parked in what was beginning to feel like *her* spot outside Graham's condo. Rob emerged just as she was approaching the door.

"It's all yours," he said, jabbing his thumb over his shoulder.

They talked briefly, synchronizing their schedules for the following day. Rob intended to apply a first coat of color early in the morning and return in the afternoon to apply a finish coat.

"Thanks a million, Rob," Holly called to his back as he headed for his pickup.

Inside, she went directly to the laundry room and emptied the dryer, removing each small garment and shaking it free of wrinkles. She matched up the outfits, making two separate stacks—Jennifer's and Justin's—then took them upstairs. After all, it was little extra effort to detour into the master bedroom.

Placing the clean clothes in two suitcases open on the floor of the walk-in closet, Holly mentally scribbled herself a note to buy children's hangers. Evidently the nanny in Jackson hadn't had the foresight to pack any.

The queen-size bed hadn't been made up that morning, not surprisingly. Graham had probably had his hands full getting his small son and daughter dressed, fed, and off to preschool, she reflected. What the heck, it would only take a couple of minutes to straighten up the covers. Then the bed would be ready for Jennifer and Justin to climb into.

"There," Holly said aloud after she'd acted on her charitable impulse. Before leaving the room, she picked up the twins' pajamas from the carpet and draped the cute garments over plumped pillows.

Voluntary domestic chores finished, she finally attended to her own business. An inspection of the smaller bedroom proved that Rob's work measured up to the usual high standard. The white primer coat had been applied evenly, covering the hunter-green paint that had been appropriate for a study.

Making use of a stepladder he'd left behind, Holly took a colored chalk and, freehandedly, created a flowing line from ceiling to baseboard on opposite walls and across the ceiling, connecting the two lines.

"Perfect!" she exclaimed with a satisfied sigh, perching on the ladder after she'd finished.

The earlier conversation with Rob came back to her. He'd been right when he zeroed in her attitude toward this decorating job, Holly mused. Her enthusiasm level *was* higher than usual. Why?

Holly pondered the question and remembered her words to Rob: *I've met the children and I fell in love with them.* It was true she felt genuine affection for Justin and Jennifer. She'd gotten almost instantly attached to them. That personal element made a difference somehow. Perhaps because she could imagine them playing and sleeping in the wonderful bedroom she visualized.

Shrugging aside her thoughts Holly pulled out her tablet. Balancing it on her knees, she hummed a tune, the same Beatles tune Rob had whistled, and worked on her sketches for the two murals she was designing.

This was such fun. Holly was just itching to get started painting the murals.

Chapter Six

"My mommy has a dress just like yours," Jennifer said, stroking the red fabric of Holly's calf-length dress. Holly hadn't bothered to go home and change clothes for the shopping trip. She wore the outfit she'd worn all day.

"It's the same color," Justin put in.

Holly looked at Graham, not quite knowing how to respond to the children's comments.

"Red was one of Heather's favorite colors," he said.

"Mine, too," she admitted.

"I noticed." His gaze went over her with reluctant admiration. All the nerve endings in Holly's body pinged to life. "I can believe she had a dress just like that. It's uncanny how your fashion sense reminds me of hers."

Great, Holly thought. This dress was almost brand-new, and now she couldn't ever enjoy wearing the darn thing again. What was she supposed to do? Get rid of her whole wardrobe? Change her "fashion sense"?

"Shall we go?" Graham prompted.

The four of them trooped outside to her minivan. Jennifer and Justin both scrambled for the window seat. When the little girl came out the loser, she typically set up a howl. To Holly's surprise, Graham got into the fray, speaking sternly to his daughter.

"Hush, Jennifer. You can have the window seat on the way home from the shopping center." She blinked, stopping midhowl, as though in shock. Immediately her eyes flooded with huge tears that spilled over and coursed wetly down her cheeks. Graham muttered a helpless curse under his breath and turned to Holly. *Now what the hell am I supposed to do?* he demanded silently.

"Stick to your guns," Holly murmured.

"Climb up into the seat, and I'll help you fasten your seat belt," he instructed Jennifer in a gruff tone.

She complied, cringing to make herself as small

as possible and averting her head so as not to look at him.

Holly stood back, watching, aching with empathy for both father and daughter. He slid the door closed and sucked in a deep breath as though fortifying himself.

"You handled that well," she said, keeping her voice low for his hearing only. Without thinking, she reached out and gave his arm an approving squeeze. He flinched, his muscles turning to steel under her palm. "Oh, for heaven's sake!" Holly exclaimed in exasperation and turned on her heel.

Graham grasped her arms from behind, stopping her before she could march around to the driver's side. "Dammit, I'm sorry," he said. "I know it's just your nature to be demonstrative."

"You're wrong. I stay awake nights plotting ways to torment you. An innocent touch on his arm should do the trick, I tell myself."

"Don't be sarcastic. Look, any physical contact with you steps up my pulse. Don't ask me why."

"It was the same way with Heather, I suppose."

"Yes."

Holly made a sound of irritation. "Maybe I should just wear surgical gloves any time I'm around you."

He sighed. "A better solution is for us not to be around each other."

"I didn't exactly twist your arm to get you to agree to this shopping trip."

"No, and I'm very grateful. I truly am." His thumbs moved on her skin, sending shivers of pleasure through her.

"That steps up *my* pulse," she informed him.

He dropped his hands fast.

"Are we going soon?" Justin called out, impatience in his young voice.

"Right now," Holly answered.

She took her time circling the minivan around the rear, giving her body a chance to cool while she recovered her perspective. Jennifer and Justin needed her on a temporary basis. And so did their dad. *Temporary* was the key word.

Who could blame Graham for being woman-shy under the circumstances? In his shoes, she probably would swear off sex and passion, too.

Considering that Holly had ruled out anything more than friendship between the two of them, it was all for the better that he keep them both in line.

On the way to the Slidell mall, Holly engaged the twins in conversation about their first day at preschool. Graham put in questions of his own, showing genuine interest. The sexual tension between him and Holly didn't dissipate entirely, but it simmered down to a manageable level.

Quite obviously a clear perspective didn't kill physical attraction.

* * *

"Are you twins?" The saleswoman who'd rung up Graham's purchases addressed his two children while he was signing a charge slip with a hefty total.

Justin answered her, nodding his head. "But I'm the oldest," he said. "I was borned first."

"You're the spitting image of your daddy." She shifted her smiling gaze to Jennifer, who shrank against Holly. "And you look just like your mother, don't you? You're pretty as a little princess."

"I'm not their mother," Holly corrected the woman pleasantly. "But if I were, I'd certainly be proud of them. They're sweet children."

"Our mommy went to heaven," Justin explained.

"Oh. I'm so sorry."

Compassionate murmurs came from several other customers who'd drifted over to the checkout counter and were waiting for service, forming a small audience.

"We live with our daddy now." The little boy apparently felt the need to elaborate.

Right on cue, Jennifer found her voice. "He's not our daddy."

By this time, Graham had finished scrawling his signature and laid down the pen on top of the slip. "Yes, I am." He contradicted his daughter in a tone that was gentle but firm.

Jennifer averted her head and didn't look at him as she replied defiantly, "Mommy didn't tell us we had a daddy."

"Nevertheless you do."

"Here's your receipt, sir," said the embarrassed saleswoman. "Thank you for shopping at our store."

Graham grabbed the several large bags. When Holly held out her hand, he gave her one. With the children in tow, they made their way toward an exit leading into the mall. Holly was bursting to express her admiration of his handling of the public scene with Jennifer.

"A+ in parenting," she said as soon as they were out of earshot of their audience. She deliberately couched her remark in words whose meaning would elude the twins.

He looked searchingly at her. "Really?"

"I wanted to applaud." Right now it was a good thing she was carrying the bag or she doubted she would be able to restrain herself. She wanted to hook her arm in his or hug him around the waist to express her surge of exuberance.

"It's an issue I had to deal with sooner or later."

"Sooner was good."

"Thanks for the supportive words. I need them."

"For a while."

He was about to answer, when Justin spoke up, announcing, "I'm hungry."

"Me, too," Jennifer said, her sulkiness vanishing.

"Make that me, three," Holly said.

Graham added his vote good-naturedly. "Make that me, four."

"We could spare your kitchen floor by having supper here at the mall," she pointed out.

"That's an inducement."

They agreed that he would take the shopping bags out to the minivan while Holly and the twins found a table in the food court. It was the closest he'd come to acting relaxed and cheerful in her presence during these last three days during which his new role of parenthood weighted him down like a too-heavy burden he was committed to carrying.

"I hope your shirt isn't ruined," Holly said as they cleared their table after supper, preparing to leave.

"Fortunately I have lots of shirts," Graham replied. "It was pretty smart of you to wear red. Spaghetti sauce blends right in."

She laughed appreciatively at his dry humor. "I knew we both were in for trouble when these two wanted spaghetti and meatballs for their supper."

During the meal she'd gotten spattered with sauce just like he had, but she hadn't shown any sign of minding. In fact, she'd seemed to enjoy herself. Graham wouldn't go as far as to say he'd enjoyed the meal, but he had actually tasted his food tonight for the first time since his life had become an ongoing trauma last Friday.

"Come on, kids," he said to the twins, who were obviously winding down.

They made their exit from the shopping mall and trooped across the parking lot to the minivan. "Want me to drive?" he offered, and Holly promptly handed over her keys.

Minutes later he turned left onto the ramp leading up to I–12.

"Mission accomplished," Graham said. "Now the twins have enough clothes, I shouldn't have to worry about doing laundry so often. Thanks for giving up your evening. Maybe I could do something for you sometime."

"It was no sacrifice. I had a good time."

"You really did seem to. You're such a good sport."

"Being a good sport implies putting up with a situation you don't especially like. That wasn't the case," she protested. "Tonight was fun. Honest."

"I can't help wondering, though—"

"It's dark outside," Jennifer said from the back seat. Her complaint was drowsy as well as querulous. "I can't see anything out the window."

"We'll be home in about twenty minutes," Graham said to his daughter. He was more glad than sorry she'd interrupted him midsentence.

Holly reached around and patted the little girl's leg. "You can see the pretty car lights, can't you?"

"Uh-huh." Her answer was muffled by a yawn. No more complaints were forthcoming.

"They're both fast asleep," Holly reported, her tone fond and tender.

"It's amazing how they can be awake one moment and zonked the next." Graham snapped his fingers. "Like that."

"Innocence and a clear conscience."

A silence fell. Graham considered resuming the interrupted conversation and decided not to.

"You were wondering about something," Holly reminded him.

He hesitated. "I'd better keep what I was wondering to myself. You might be offended."

"It wouldn't be the first time. Tell me."

"Okay. My question is how much does novelty play into your enjoyment of Justin and Jennifer? I see mothers out with their children and not many of them are as patient as you. Though you probably remind me more of a big sister the way you relate to Justin and Jennifer," he added, struck by the insight. "Maybe because you enter into the spirit of their games."

"And big sisters can go off and do something else when the novelty of playing with cute younger siblings wears off. Is that your point?"

She'd zeroed in on what was bothering him. "Yes."

"The new wears off everything. But I don't think I would get bored with your children after I was around them a few weeks or a few months. In fact, I'm sure I wouldn't. I'm not bored with my work after being an interior decorator for seven years."

"True, but you're dealing with different clients, not the same ones over and over. Actually there's continuous newness. Constant challenge. The same as in my work as an architect."

"Relationships with people aren't static just like careers aren't static. Not the relationships that endure. I still have friends from grade school. Friends from high school. Friends from college. Several cousins and I get together every year at the beach." Her voice had been growing more and more indignant. "I'm *not* a shallow person, for your information."

"I *didn't* mean to imply you are," Graham hastened to assure her. "The last thing I want to do is insult you." Now he wished he'd kept his mouth shut.

"Well, I am insulted, for the nth time. Just because I wear red and remind you of Heather, you figure my affection for your children is superficial."

"I don't think that." Or did he?

"If things were different and you and I got along, I'd love to adopt Jennifer and Justin as the niece and nephew I'll never have, since I'm an only child and I don't plan on marrying. But don't worry, I realize that's not in the cards.''

"So as soon as you finish up their bedroom, you'll say goodbye to them?''

"Isn't that what you want?''

Graham had come up behind a slow-moving automobile. He put on the turn signal and passed a line of cars, delaying answering until he'd pulled over into the right lane of the interstate again. "I'm not so self-involved that I'd deprive Justin and Jennifer of having you as a surrogate aunt.''

"If my desire to be a surrogate aunt is really genuine, you mean.''

"Consider it an option is what I mean.''

"Good. I will.'' She fell silent. Somewhat to his surprise, her silence wasn't brooding.

Finally curiosity got the best of him and he worked up his nerve to ask, "Penny for your thoughts?''

"I wondered what you thought of a trip to Disney World with the twins. I've always wanted to go.''

Graham could tell she wasn't being facetious. "Something puzzles me,'' he said.

"Give me a second to put on my armor. Okay. What other flaw in my character puzzles you?''

He ignored her sarcasm. "If you have no problem maintaining long-term relationships with friends and cousins, why are you so leery of marriage?''

"Because I don't live with my friends and cousins. They don't expect me to give up my social life and my career and cater full-time to them.''

"Not all men expect their wives to give up careers and cater to them.''

"True, but that's the view of marriage I got, growing up. Every time my mother remarried, she had to rearrange her whole routine to suit her latest husband. And my father was just as demanding of each of his wives.'' Holly shivered. "I swore when I was twelve I wasn't ever getting married and giving up my freedom to be me.''

"Haven't you known married couples who were happy and fulfilled?''

"Precious few. Most of the time when I become well acquainted with husbands or wives, they eventually start to complain about their spouses and confide their dissatisfactions. Don't you experience the same thing?''

"I take those complaints with a grain of salt. But then my background is completely different from yours. My parents have a good marriage.'' In the interest of candor, Graham felt compelled to add, "Of course, my brother, Greg, is divorced, as I've already mentioned.''

"The statistics say it all, I'm afraid. Marriages don't last. Still, the majority of adults keep repeating the vows to different mates, trying for that combination that clicks.'' She herself wouldn't ever buy into such foolish optimism, Holly's tone of voice clearly implied.

Graham couldn't explain why her strong anti-marriage bias would cause him to feel despondent.

But it did.

They let the subject drop. A few minutes later Holly tuned in a radio talk show on a popular New Orleans station. Conversation for the rest of the drive to Mandeville consisted of responding to the views of callers who had their say on the topic of the evening: Solving the traffic problem on the Lake Pontchartrain Causeway, a twenty-four-mile-long bridge with two spans connecting the North Shore to the South Shore.

''The best solution is find a job or start a business on the North Shore, and don't commute,'' Holly stated.

''I agree.''

They were pretty much in accord with their other comments, too, including labeling some callers as idiots. Graham's morose mood lifted, and he'd begun to feel more upbeat as he parked her minivan in his driveway.

Holly seemed to assume that she would go inside instead of telling him good-night and leaving. Graham wasn't about to try to get rid of her. He welcomed her help in getting the two sleepy children into their pajamas and tucking them into bed.

Who was he kidding? He also welcomed her company whether that was wise or unwise.

Fortunately, Jennifer was too drowsy to protest his carrying her as well as her brother. The little girl curled her arm around Graham's neck and nestled her cheek on his shoulder just like Justin did on the opposite shoulder.

"You have an armload," Holly said, walking beside him with shopping bags in both hands. "Together they must weigh sixty pounds."

"Every bit of it."

Graham found it odd that bearing the deadweight of the two small, lax bodies was enjoyable in some way he couldn't quite explain. And strangely, his burden of responsibility didn't weigh quite so heavily as it had during the past four days. He could almost believe that being a father might have its rewarding moments.

"Keys are in my right pocket," he said when they reached the front door.

Holly slipped her hand inside his pants pocket. He didn't mind her doing it.

Not at all.

"I can manage this by myself," Holly whispered. "Why don't you go downstairs and watch the news or something?"

"Give me the scissors. I'll remove the tags," Graham whispered back, holding out his hand.

Holly had taken upon herself the task of putting away the new clothing, folding the small garments neatly and placing them in two open suitcases. He'd squatted down beside her in his walk-in closet. The twins were sound asleep in his queen-size bed.

"You smell like spaghetti sauce," she objected. Her real objection was that the sizable closet seemed much too small, much too private. Plus, she liked having him share the limited space with her far too much.

"Hold on a second. I'll take off this shirt."

"Don't—"

But he was already jerking the shirttails out of his trousers. Holly carefully removed another tag, exercising every ounce of willpower not to watch him as he rapidly undid buttons.

"There," he said after he'd stripped off the shirt and thrown it out into the bedroom.

Darn it. Holly was human. She turned her head and checked him out. No disappointing surprises. His T-shirts had already clued her in on his great build from the waist up. She'd guessed he had a liberal growth of dark hair on his chest. And he did, sure enough. Her fingers itched to touch the springy curls. A shivery sensation slid down her spine.

Sex alarm. Do something, Holly, she told herself.

"I still smell spaghetti sauce." She wrinkled up her nose. "It's on my dress. And on your pants."

"I'd better not take my pants off."

"Not a good idea," Holly agreed. She met his gaze and went weak with desire, reading the hot, frank message in his eyes. *I'd like nothing better than to get naked with you.* It was up to her to cool them both down. "Graham, I suggest you grab a shirt and let me finish up here. Otherwise we'll start something we shouldn't." She'd strived for a no-nonsense tone.

"Maybe we should start something," he said, his voice deep and urgent. "I sure want to bad enough."

"That's your body talking, not your brain." Holly scrambled to her feet. Actions were her only course now, words having failed. "You finish up. I'm going home."

He didn't plead with her to stay.

Luckily he hadn't used any physical persuasion. He hadn't touched her or kissed her. If he had, Holly didn't doubt for a minute she would have been lost to reason. They would probably have shed their clothes and made wild, passionate love right there on the closet floor.

Darn, it was hard to be glad that hadn't happened.

Chapter Seven

Holly always loved returning to her house in Madisonville, but tonight the sense of homecoming was especially strong. Turning into the driveway, she braked at an angle, letting her headlights illuminate the front porch with its fancy railing of elaborately turned stiles. She absolutely adored the porch, adored the gingerbread trim, adored the steep angles of the roof.

A previous owner, who'd renovated the Victorian cottage built in the 1930s, had painted it pristine white with apricot trim. Holly hadn't changed the colors, deeming them perfect, like a prissy, becoming dress. She even described her house to people as "prissy."

"It's so prissy and adorable! You just want to hug it!" she'd exclaimed to friends when she'd first discovered it.

Holly related to buildings and things with exuberant emotion. She regularly "fell in love" with pieces of furniture and accent items. The spring wreath decorating her door, for example. She'd seen it and simply *had* to buy it for herself. The combination of plain brown grapevines wound into a homely, irregular circle and bright silk tulips was soul satisfying. Holly *loved* that wreath.

But she might sell it tomorrow to a client or neighbor or even a stranger who came along and wanted it desperately. Because there was surely another wonderful wreath out there. Ownership of almost anything she acquired could turn out to be temporary. As much as she adored her house, she didn't think for a minute she'd hang on to it for the rest of her life.

That didn't make her superficial. Did it?

Graham would probably come to that conclusion, she reflected, sighing. No doubt Heather had recycled her possessions, too.

Inside the house, Holly listened to her voice mail. Among the twenty or so messages, half a dozen had been left by friends wanting her to do something social with them. Fun things she would definitely enjoy. Patricia Connors read her an excerpt from a movie review and asked Holly to call so they could make a date to see the movie when Patricia's husband was out of town. Jimmy Lott, her art show buddy, reminded her of an upcoming event in the sister town of Covington when all the small art galleries would open their doors for a wine-and-cheese party. He, too, requested a call to firm up a date.

There was also a party invitation. A lunch invitation. An invitation to join two gay men friends, also former clients, on an excursion to New Orleans to poke around in antique shops on Magazine Street.

It took Holly forty-five minutes to respond to the messages and make all the dates. She ended up chatting with each person. No sooner had she hung up after the final call than she heard a knock on her back door. Her next-door neighbor, Agatha Linn, had baked an angel food cake and brought Holly a slice along with a container of fresh strawberries for topping and another container with homemade chocolate sauce. A divorced woman in her forties with two teenage boys, Agatha was an attorney. She was also a gourmet cook.

"Come in and visit a while," Holly urged. "I'll make some coffee."

The cake was to die for. Holly savored every morsel while Agatha entertained her with a witty account of a recent court trial.

Closing the door after bidding her departing neighbor good-night, Holly paused to reflect on her good fortune. I'm so lucky. I have a full, happy life. Good neighbors, lots of friends, a career I love. At the present moment she wasn't dating anyone, but there was barely a void.

Well, a small void.

Still, this single lifestyle suited her perfectly. She would feel smothered in a marriage. Holly just knew she would. She'd made the right decision when she was twelve and vowed never to follow in the path her mother had taken. A path so common these days. Marriage, divorce, remarriage. It was practically the norm.

Holly shuddered.

In her bedroom she removed the red dress, catching a whiff of spaghetti sauce. The scent transported her to the food court at the shopping mall and supper with Graham and the twins. Justin and Jennifer were so adorable and fun to be around. And their daddy was such a fine man, in addition to being a hunk. She liked and admired him. She was strongly attracted to him, too, of course. Understatement of the year.

Would she see him tomorrow? See the twins? She hoped so.

Holly dropped the dress onto a pile of garments destined for the dry cleaner's, conscious that her earlier complacency had vanished and now she felt wistful. Incomplete. Almost lonely. And Holly never felt lonely.

It was just a passing mood and would be gone when she woke up in the morning with a million things to do, she told herself.

Graham sat in the closet on his haunches a full minute after Holly had fled. He needed the cold-shower remedy. But first he'd finish up the job he'd interrupted when he'd joined her and immediately got turned on by her nearness.

She'd kept her head, which might or might not be a good thing. Graham frankly wasn't sure at this point. All he knew was how much he wanted her. The sexual tension kept building for him every time they were together. Maybe making love would dispel that tension. He guessed he was more willing to take that avenue than the alternative, which was keeping away from her entirely.

After all, neither of them was wide-eyed and innocent. Graham figured he was more at risk than she was, but he wouldn't let himself fall in love with her. She'd made it clear she wasn't any more interested in a husband than Heather had been.

Although her espousing that attitude might be some kind of trick. How could he ever believe any woman again?

Using Holly's small scissors, Graham clipped the rest of the tags and folded the small outfits. His heartbeat slowed to normal and his state of hard arousal eased.

After scooping up all the bits of cardboard, Graham took the double handful into the bedroom and dumped the tags in a wastebasket. Remembering the scissors, he retrieved them and stuck them, handles down, in a rear pocket of his slacks. It wouldn't do to leave the scissors where the twins could find them. They might seriously injure themselves.

The thought awoke anxiety. Graham assumed it was parental anxiety, and would dog him from now on.

He glanced at the bed and saw that Jennifer had rolled all the way to the edge. If she moved any farther, she would topple onto the floor. Graham walked around to her side, eased his arms under her small lax form and placed her nearer the center.

She smiled in her sleep while he was still bent over.

Maybe one of these days his little daughter would get over her dislike and smile at him, he reflected, touching her cheek gently with his fingertip.

Justin had kicked off the sheet. Graham went around to his side of the bed and covered the little boy. In the interest of not showing partiality, he stroked Justin's cheek lightly, too.

At the doorway Graham paused and looked back. So far, so good. Jennifer slept exactly where he'd repositioned her. Justin was still covered. They were as safe as Graham could ensure for the time being.

He'd gotten through day four of being a father. With lots of help from Holly.

Downstairs, Graham put the scissors out of sight on a high shelf. He would leave a note for Holly and tell her where to find them. She would be here tomorrow to unlock the door for the painter. Surprising how comfortable he was with the idea of her coming and going at will, Graham thought as he turned on the TV to do some channel surfing until the ten o'clock news came on.

Following the news, he prepared his makeshift bed on the sofa. Tonight there was no tossing and turning. Not long after his head had hit the pillow, he fell soundly asleep.

The next thing Graham knew, the living room was flooded with the pale light of early morning. It was six o'clock, the time he'd been used to rising when he had no inkling he was a father.

He'd slept through the night, without waking up once.

"I'm sorry, Graham," Angela said, gazing at him regretfully. "I can't help you out, not this afternoon. I'm taking Ricky to the doctor. He's developing another ear infection."

Ricky was Angela's seven-year-old, her middle child.

"Don't worry. I'll figure out something," Graham assured his secretary.

"Isn't there a neighbor who can pick up the twins at preschool?" she asked.

"Not really." He was on a first-name basis with his neighbors, but he couldn't ask this kind of favor of any of them. Plus, he didn't want to dispatch a complete stranger to collect Jennifer and Justin.

"What are you going to do?" she asked. "Mr. Cleveland insisted you be present at the meeting with the general contractor at five o'clock. On the phone he sounded fit to be tied."

"For good reason. His office building is running way over budget, thanks to the sudden rise in prices of some of the building materials." Such problems all went with the territory of being an architect.

"It's too bad you don't have family close by to turn to, in a pinch."

"I'll figure out something," Graham said again. He turned the conversation to business matters and gave Angela some instructions before he left the office to go to a building site in a subdivision and inspect the progress of a house under construction.

So what *was* he going to do? he asked himself, striding toward his pickup outside.

The answer was pretty damn obvious. Call Holly and ask her if she could pick up the twins and look after them for an hour or two.

Graham tried Holly's home phone number on his

cell phone. An answering machine clicked on. He muttered a curse of exasperation, checking for traffic and pulling out onto the street. Great. Holly wasn't there. He listened to the message in her lilting voice and admitted to himself that as much as he hated to ask a favor, he was glad for an excuse to see her later on today. She recited her beeper number and cell phone number.

He repeated both aloud, memorizing them. After going the beeper routine, he tried the cell phone. No luck. Suppressing his frustration, he turned up the volume on his radio. It was tuned to the same station that had aired the talk show last night. The memory of riding home from the mall with Holly came back.

She not only was vivacious and sexy, she was an interesting, bright woman. But Heather had been interesting and bright, too, Graham recalled. He'd been blind to her secret agenda and had become so infatuated that he'd asked her to marry him. Holly seemed honest, but maybe he was being taken for a sucker again. For all he knew, she might have some agenda herself.

Graham didn't plan to lose sight of that possibility.

Ten minutes into his journey, he tried Holly's home-and-business phone again. Then her cell phone. Still no luck. Where was she? A couple of times at the mall she'd answered calls on her cell phone. Surely she kept it with her during business hours so that she was accessible to clients and others needing to contact her.

He braked for a red light, glancing over to his left at a health club he'd designed two years ago. The parking lot was jammed. He'd tried to tell the owner the space wasn't adequate.

Was that Holly's minivan parked next to the bright red convertible? Graham stared, feeling his heartbeat pick up speed.

A horn tooted lightly behind him. The light had changed to green. He wasn't in the left-turn lane, so he had to accelerate. The minivan probably belonged to someone else, but it was worth a few extra minutes to backtrack and find out, Graham decided.

It *was* hers.

He recognized the number on the license plate and also spotted a tiny dent on the rear. Still, just to be absolutely positive, Graham got out of his pickup in the club parking lot and peered into the minivan. Yep. Wallpaper books and carpet samples. Luck was with him. He'd accidentally tracked Holly down.

Now if he could locate a parking spot.

Minutes later Graham entered the front door and signed in as a visitor at the check-in desk. He knew the layout of the club. Thanks to the fact that he'd designed it with a lot of plate-glass interior walls, all he had to do was stroll past workout rooms and racquetball courts and studios for exercise classes and glance at the people in search of Holly.

He spotted her in one of the latter. Even with the doors closed, he could hear a fast rock-and-roll song and feel the throb of the bass and instruments. It was one of those dance-to-high-energy-music classes. Thirty or so women inside the room were whirling and gyrating and doing high kicks along with the instructor, but Graham had eyes only for Holly.

His gut reaction was a male *wow*. She was sexy enough in regular clothes, but the sight of her in black leggings and a form-hugging leotard that looked like it had been inspired by an artist's palette with dabs of bright paint, made his mouth go dry. And affected the rest of him, too.

The song ended and so did the routine. A woman next to Holly said something to her and pointed. Toward Graham. Holly glanced at him, and he smiled and waved at her, embarrassed because he was standing with his nose practically pressed to the plate glass wall. Obviously he'd attracted the attention of Holly's fellow exercise-group member.

Holly pointed to herself, pantomiming the question, *Are you here to see me?*

Graham nodded vigorously while he made an apologetic gesture with his hands, pantomiming, *Sorry to interrupt.*

She scooped up a towel and was dabbing at perspiration as she joined him out in the corridor.

"That's quite a workout," he said, his gaze following the progress of the towel. The flushed warmth of her body seemed to hit him in an arousing wave.

"It's great. I love it. I get bored with plain old exercise."

"You're as good as the instructor." Graham immediately felt dishonest because he hadn't watched the instructor enough to make a comparison.

"Not quite. Kiki has danced professionally."

Graham drew in a deep breath. The twins. He was here to make arrangements for them. "I was driving by and noticed your van. I'd been trying to get you on the phone."

"I leave my beeper and cell phone in the locker room. The music would drown them out anyway." She was dabbing her cleavage, a job he wished he could do for her. "What's up?"

My blood pressure, Graham answered silently. "I'm in kind of a bind." He explained his problem.

"You want me to pick up the twins." She reached the conclusion for herself, saving him from having to word the request. "Sure. I can do that. You'll need to notify the preschool."

"Will do." She was lifting up her hair with one hand and patting the nape of her neck with the towel, in the process also lifting her high, firm breasts. Graham dragged his gaze back to her face, but not before he'd taken note of her nipples probing the leotard. "I really appreciate this, Holly."

"Don't consider it a favor to you. I'll enjoy a few hours with Justin and Jennifer."

"Those two will be tickled when you show up instead of me. I'm sure of that."

She excused herself and slipped back inside the studio. The exercise group was in the midst of another energetic routine. Graham watched Holly a couple of minutes, subjecting himself to as much torment as pleasure, before he tore himself away.

Passing the locker room, he mentally stepped into a cold shower he needed nearly as much he'd needed one last night.

Back on the highway, Graham was jarred by a realization. The scene with Holly in the health club hadn't brought the disturbing sense of déjà vu that it should have. Heather had been wearing a leotard that popped his eyeballs when he met her at the health club in Mandeville where he was a member. She'd taken exercise classes, he knew, although he'd never observed her during a class. She'd also worked out on the machines when he was working out, but, after the fact, he would just bet she had been bored by "plain old exercise," too, Graham reflected bitterly.

So many parallels. It was enough to make him wonder if Holly wasn't really Heather's secret twin, out to ensnare him all over again, just for the pure hell of it.

"Something smells good." Graham said, following the food aroma to his kitchen when he walked in the door that evening.

"It's roasted chicken," Jennifer informed him.

Justin recited the rest of the supper menu. "And peas and carrots. And green salad from the salad bar."

"We helped Holly pick out the brownest chicken at the supermarket deli," Jennifer explained.

"And helped her set the table. Didn't we, Holly?" Graham's son turned to Holly confidently for confirmation.

She smiled warmly at the little boy and at his sister. "You and Jennifer were a big help."

Graham had called Holly during the afternoon to tell her he would pick up supper on his way home, but she'd pointed out his meeting might run late. It only made sense for her to buy supper. He'd gratefully agreed.

"Thanks to all three of you," he said now. "This is awfully nice, especially as hungry as I am." It *was* nice, damned nice coming home to find her there, the children happy and everything under control.

"Did your meeting go well?" Holly inquired.

"Very well. We came up with some modifications to keep costs in line with the budget without sacrificing too much quality.'' He was washing his hands at the sink while he answered. ''What can I do?''

''You can carve the chicken. I'll serve the vegetables and salad.''

They were about to sit down at the table when Graham remembered the booster seats in his truck. He snapped his fingers. ''I forgot something. Be right back.''

''Those are cute!'' Holly exclaimed on his return. She came over to him and took one of the varnished wooden seats and examined it. ''You had them made?''

''By a golfing buddy of mine who's a cabinetmaker. C.J. Bates. I described what I needed and he did them as a rush job.''

''I know C.J. He's a fine craftsman. Look, Jennifer and Justin. Your names are carved into your own special seats. Isn't that fun?''

''Personalizing them was C.J.'s inspiration,'' Graham felt compelled to admit. Now he wished it had been his own. He might have scored more points with her.

The supper was the first meal that Graham actually enjoyed since the delivery of the twins last Friday. Evidently he was adjusting to family meals with a couple of three-and-a-half-year-olds. Both children ate well and, miraculously, neither toppled over his or her glass of milk. True, quite a few peas and carrot pieces found their way to the floor. During the clean-up afterward Graham knelt down without comment and collected them in his palm.

"Maybe you need a dog," Holly said. She was wiping the table with a damp sponge.

"One with a garbage-hound pedigree?" He was rewarded with her amused laughter.

Jennifer and Justin made it plain they expected Holly to stay and assist with their baths. She did so, seemingly with pleasure, once again making the nighttime routine easy for Graham. And fun for the twins.

That was the keynote. She made everything fun for them. Because she was entertaining herself, too. But how long before the novelty faded?

Don't get used to this, Graham told himself sternly. One day soon she'll tire of the twins. Tire of you.

"How about a glass of wine? I promise I won't go to sleep on you tonight."

"Thanks, but I'd better go." Holly had rehearsed a refusal, knowing one wouldn't come naturally to her lips.

"Do you have to? We can check out what's playing on the movie channels."

"There's a Mel Gibson movie, I know. In the

supermarket I overheard someone say that it was coming on tonight.''

"Great. I like his action flicks. Make yourself comfortable. I'll be right back."

Holly's intentions to leave and avoid being alone with him evaporated. Mainly because she neither wanted to leave or avoid his company.

He returned in less than five minutes carrying two filled wineglasses. The TV was playing, and she'd kicked off her shoes and was curled up at one end of the sofa.

"Good. You found the remote control. These days that's a challenge,'' he said with good-natured irony.

As soon as he'd sat down, the cordless phone on an end table near Holly rang. She lifted the phone from the cradle and handed it to him. The caller was his mother, it was easy to surmise from his end of the conversation. Holly knew he'd been in communication with his parents about his sudden parenthood because he'd told her as much.

"Hi, Mom... Things are going okay, I guess. I'm coping... No, it's not an easy adjustment. For me or for the kids... This weekend? Sure. Saturday or Sunday?" Graham looked over at Holly while he was listening to the reply. His expression became thoughtful. "Sunday, then. Oh, and I might bring a friend, Holly Beaumont, if she doesn't already have plans... No, I'm not dating her. She's someone I've known a while and I've had to turn to her for help... See you Sunday. And say hi to Dad... Bye, Mom.''

Holly had almost choked on a sip of wine at his mention of her. He and his mother presumably had been arranging a first meeting between the twins and their paternal grandparents. And Graham wanted to include Holly?

"That was my mother, obviously," he said, laying the phone on the coffee table. "She invited the twins and me for Sunday dinner at their place in Picayune, Mississippi. You're included in the invitation."

"I heard you include me." Why on earth had he?

"My parents are pretty interesting people. I don't think you'd find them boring. Plus, my mom's an outstanding cook. We'll have a delicious meal. And it's not a bad drive, about an hour and fifteen minutes. They have a ranch. With horses," he added as though the information might be an inducement.

"Are you nervous about making the drive with the twins by yourself?"

"Not as nervous as I would have been just a few days ago. They're getting to be better passengers with me."

Still, he was uneasy about that long a drive, Holly could tell.

"I suppose my presence might put Justin and Jennifer more at ease in a strange setting."

"Without a doubt. But don't feel obligated. You've done so much already."

"It's important they bond with their new grandparents." She was talking herself into going along.

"I feel fairly confident that will happen. Over time."

But Holly might speed up the process. Sunday was only one day out of her life. "You can count me in. I'd like to go," she said.

It was the truth. She *did* want to accompany him and his children to his parents' house, Holly acknowledged with inner amazement. And a touch of concern over her own motivations.

"Fantastic," Graham said.

The movie came on. It was action packed, and Holly got absorbed in the story. Not absorbed enough that she wasn't pleasurably aware of Graham close by, every bit as appealing and masculine as Mel Gibson. At some point after she and Graham had both put down their empty wineglasses, he took her hand and linked his fingers with hers. Holding hands with him was nice. Really nice.

"I'm glad I stayed and watched that," she said when the credits were rolling following a dramatic finale. "I liked it. Didn't you?"

"A lot." He squeezed her hand.

"There's a drawback to no commercial breaks, though."

Comprehension took a second. "No bathroom break, you mean. Damn. I was about to try to steal a kiss." He went ahead and stole one anyway. His lips were warm and firm.

"Nice," Holly murmured, sighing her pleasure. "Would you excuse me?"

He got up, too, and picked up the wineglasses. A few minutes later when she came out of the powder room, she found him in the kitchen. He didn't try to dissuade her from leaving, but he kissed her good-night, a longer, more passionate kiss that left them both short of breath.

"Sooner or later," Graham said, his voice husky, "it's got to happen."

Holly didn't pretend not to understand he was referring to their eventually making love. "But do you think it *should* happen?" she asked.

"You don't, obviously. Or at least that's the way I'm reading you."

"Things are so complicated by the similarity between Heather and me. While we were kissing just now, a part of me was wondering, *Is he kissing you or a Heather look-alike?*"

"I wasn't thinking about Heather," he denied.

"But you might be attracted to me because I resemble her, right?"

"This all gets a little deep for me. I'm no psychologist."

Holly sighed. "Me, either. Why don't we just stick to being friends? Don't you agree that's wise, under the circumstances?"

"Wise, sure. Realistic?" He shrugged his skepticism. "Right now, even after this discussion, if I had a bedroom to take you to..." The hot desire in his eyes acted like foreplay for Heather. Her breasts felt heavy and her knees literally went weak. And there were other erotic physical symptoms. Much more unsettling was a different effect his incomplete statement had on her. The note of yearning in his voice awoke that alien sense of incompleteness she'd felt last night, thinking about him.

"Good night, Graham." Holly was headed for the door.

"Good night. Oh, wait. I owe you money for supper."

"Pay me another time."

She got out of there, obeying a panicky instinct that said, *Run, don't walk, to the nearest exit.*

Chapter Eight

"Why isn't Holly eating supper with us?" Jennifer asked plaintively as Graham and his children took their places at the table.

"She was going to a movie tonight. Remember, I already explained that to you and Justin several times." Graham kept his voice patient. He empathized with his daughter's dissatisfaction. She and her brother missed Holly's warm, sunny presence. So did their father.

"Tell me about preschool," Graham said, forking a bite of macaroni and cheese, which he guessed he'd better learn to enjoy often. Earlier he'd done what he thought Holly would approve of, by inviting the twins' input on the supper menu. They'd said in unison, "Macaroni and cheese." Graham hadn't succeeded in talking them into another food choice.

"I played with Jimmy and a little boy named Mike today," Justin said. "Mike's littler than me. He's only this tall." The little boy held his hand in a horizontal position at his neck.

Should I correct the grammar error and suggest "smaller" as a better description than "littler?" Graham wondered. Or would that be an error in parenting? Damn if he knew. He made a mental note to ask Holly.

"How about you, Jennifer? Who did you play with at preschool?" Graham questioned his daughter, who hadn't offered any response.

She hunched small shoulders in a shrug and didn't answer.

"Jennifer mostly plays by herself," Justin offered, his mouth full of macaroni.

"I like to play by myself. Those other kids don't play right." She dropped her spoon to her plate with a loud clatter.

Graham realized his little daughter was upset by the conversation. He was upset himself. His clear vision of a whole group of children busily interacting and Jennifer an isolated outsider dismayed him. Tomorrow he would make it his business to talk to the director of the preschool and share his concerns with her.

But what wise words could he speak to Jennifer right this minute to make her feel good about herself?

"I'll bet Jennifer will have some playmates, too, once she decides she'd rather not play by herself," he stated, reaching over to give her arm a gentle squeeze. She looked at him, big blue eyes mirroring uncertainty. He smiled reassuringly.

Graham couldn't have been any more gratified when Jennifer resumed eating her supper. He felt as though he'd passed an important milestone and earned a small amount of childish trust.

"What kind of rating would you give this movie?" asked Patricia as the theater lights came on.

"One and a half. I was disappointed," replied Holly. "My attention kept wandering." She'd kept thinking about Graham and the twins.

"Mine, too."

The two women rose from their seats. They'd sat through the credits, avoiding the rush to the exit by fellow moviegoers.

"I thought the problem might be me," Patricia said, moving toward the nearest aisle. "I have some heavy-duty stuff going on in my life."

"What?" Holly asked, immediately concerned.

"Roger and I are getting a divorce."

"You're not serious?"

"'Fraid so. I'll fill you in on the nitty-gritty details over a cup of coffee."

"Patricia, I'm so sorry."

"Yeah, me, too."

Holly hated the sense of déjà vu. How many times had she lent a sympathetic ear as friends, both women and men, confided the distressing stories of the breakup of their marriages?

Fifteen minutes later she and Patricia were doctoring their coffee to taste in a nearby restaurant.

"I sense you're not really shocked by my news," the other woman commented.

Holly sighed. "Maybe because sooner or later, most of my married friends become divorced friends." Then married friends again. "Have you and Roger considered counseling?"

"Are you kidding?" Patricia's voice rang with bitterness. "Roger's madly in love. All those long business trips he's been taking the last year? He was actually out of state about half of those days and spent the rest of the time with his girlfriend in New Orleans."

"This must hurt so much." Holly reached over and touched Patricia's arm, conveying her deep compassion for the other woman's pain. "How did you find out?"

She didn't really want to know, but experience

told her Patricia needed to pour out the tawdry tale to sympathetic ears. It was a step in the healing process.

One cup of coffee led to two. A rich dessert seemed in order as comfort food, so Holly summoned the waitress over. She had cheesecake and Patricia chose a rich chocolate concoction.

"Thanks for letting me vent," Patricia said when they'd called it a night and were outside the restaurant. "I feel like I talked out a lot of the hurt and anger. Roger was gone so much that being separated isn't going to be all that drastic a change in my life."

Holly gave her a supportive—and sincere—pep talk, once again experiencing the depressing sense of déjà vu. She didn't have enough fingers and toes to count all the times she'd bolstered friends who were facing single life again.

I need somebody to cheer me up, Holly thought as she drove away. Even allowing for sympathy, her mood was more bleak than she could explain. She honestly believed Patricia would get along fine and was well rid of Roger, in the long run.

So why was Holly so down in the dumps because another ill-fated marriage was down the tubes?

It wasn't such a hard question. The reason had something to do with Graham, she suspected. Getting to know him better had probably sparked just the tiniest hope that she was too cynical about marriage. It made her heartsick to realize all over again she should stick to her resolve to stay single and avoid what Patricia was going through.

At home she listened to her voice mail. There was a message from Graham. The sound of his voice almost instantly cured the worst of her despondency.

"Hi, Graham here. I called in case you'd gotten home from your movie by now. Nothing all that important to say other than I might have made a small breakthrough with Jennifer tonight. She and Justin are in bed asleep and I was sitting here, thinking about you. Hope you had an enjoyable evening and a dinner other than macaroni and cheese."

The last part, spoken with wry amusement, brought a smile to Holly's face. It was ten-fifteen. Too late to call him back? No, she decided, and acted quickly before she could analyze her actions to death.

"You sound awake," she said in response to his hello.

"I was watching the news. How was the movie?"

"Boring. I don't recommend it. The whole evening turned out to be a bummer. Normally my movie-buff, friend, Patricia, and I go somewhere for coffee and hash over the film we've seen. But she just split with her husband.''

''So you hashed him over instead?''

''We hashed him pretty thoroughly,'' Holly admitted. ''Step one of recovery.''

''What's step two?''

''The injured party reaches the state of mind where she or he shares some of the blame for the underlying problems that led to a breakup.''

''And step three?''

''Coming to the realization that both parties are better off calling it quits.''

''You sound like quite an expert on the subject of divorce.''

''Unfortunately I am an expert. I've gone through five divorces altogether with my parents and umpteen more with relatives and friends. It's very depressing. I get to feeling like a psychic, reading the signs of a marriage headed for the rocks.''

''In Patricia's case, you saw her breakup coming?''

''Oh, yes. I prayed I was wrong, for once. But enough on that topic. Tell me about what happened with you and Jennifer tonight.''

He recounted the earlier scene at the supper table. Holly was able to visualize it clearly. While she listened with keen interest, she found herself wishing she'd been there.

Wishing it intensely.

* * *

"I'll be out of the office a couple of hours, Angela." Graham's secretary had just returned from her lunch break, and he was about to leave. "After I grab some lunch, I plan to drop by several building sites. Beep me if something important comes up."

"That new restaurant where I ate today is great," she said. "The lunch crowd should have thinned out by now, if you're in the mood to try it."

"Probably not today," he said. "I might just go home and fix a sandwich."

Graham had every intention of swinging by his condo, whether or not he opted to go inside. The big draw wasn't lunch, but to stop and see Holly, if she happened to be there, working on the twins' bedroom. The painter had finished his job yesterday. Last night on the phone Holly had mentioned that she planned to start on the murals today.

Turning onto his street, Graham craned his neck and was rewarded for his trouble: Holly's minivan sat in his driveway. Good, he thought. Although *good* didn't quite express his surge of anticipation.

If she hadn't eaten lunch, Graham would invite her to that new restaurant Angela had gone to on Gerard Street, he decided, parking his truck behind her vehicle.

The front door was unlocked. Graham entered and walked quickly through the foyer and into the living room, where he paused, hearing a sound coming from the direction of the kitchen. Was that the clothes dryer?

"Holly," he called out, not wanting to take her by surprise and possibly give her a scare.

No answer.

After a brief hesitation, Graham passed through the kitchen and came to the door of the laundry room. Sure enough, the dryer was in use. He lifted the lid of the laundry hamper. Empty. Holly had washed a load of clothes to help him out, which was damn nice of her.

Now he had good reason to insist on taking her to lunch as a payback.

"Holly." Graham called out her name again from the living room as he headed toward the stairs. No answer. Surely she heard him.

He bounded up the stairs. The door to the smaller bedroom stood open. From the threshold of the bedroom, Graham was able to solve the mystery immediately. Holly was standing on a small stepladder, large artist's brush in hand, her back to him. She wore earphones and he figured her music was turned up loud enough to drown out noises.

Graham took a second to enjoy the rear view of her figure in snug-fitting jeans. While he was gazing at her shapely bottom, she began swaying her hips in a sexy dance. She'd finished a brush stroke and was surveying her handiwork, oblivious to his presence. Oblivious to the effect she was having on him, best described as instant turn-on.

"Hi," Graham said loudly, walking over toward her. "You've got company."

His mouth went too dry for speech when she raised both arms and wiggled her hips to the rhythm he couldn't hear. But he recognized the lyrics of an Ike and Tina Turner classic rock song when she began singing aloud, still wiggling as uninhibitedly as Tina Turner had in filmed concert performances he'd seen.

"Don't do that," Graham groaned. He reached her and touched her on the shoulder, addressing her loudly, "Hi, Holly!"

She shrieked, flung the brush and a small paint container into the air and whirled around all in one series of surprised reactions. Her feet lost contact with the narrow stepladder and she pitched forward toward Graham. He acted instinctively, grabbing her to keep her from taking a nasty spill. The force of her weight sent him staggering and he lost the battle to keep his balance. He went down, his arms tightening around her and cushioning her fall as she landed on top of him.

"I'm sorry I startled you," he said, but it was difficult to feel any genuine regret over his situation. He hadn't hurt himself and she was safe, lying on top of him, curvaceous and warm. Her heartbeat pulsed into his chest.

"Are you okay?" she asked breathlessly, raising up and gazing at him with concern. The earphones were askew.

"Couldn't be better. I kept calling out, but you didn't hear me."

"The radio station I was listening to was playing classic rock."

He grinned. "You do a mean imitation of Tina Turner."

She blushed, smiling sheepishly as she removed the earphones and tossed them aside. "How embarrassing that you've stumbled onto one of my secret fantasies. I always wanted to be a rock singer and perform in front of huge crowds at concerts."

"Really? You're not pulling my leg?"

"When I was a little girl, I got a toy microphone for Christmas one year. I spent hours practicing."

"Did you ever sing with a rock band?"

"You heard me sing just now. I can't carry a tune in a basket."

"I would buy a ticket to your concert." His tone came out husky and sincere.

"That's sweet." She leaned down and planted a tender kiss on his mouth.

Graham's embrace tightened at the explosion of sensations in his body coupled with emotion that swelled his chest. He rolled sideways, placing her on her back. Now he was looking down at her in kissing range.

"Graham, I dropped a plastic cup of paint." The reminder held regret. She was gazing at him hungrily, too. "It may seep through the drop cloth and ruin your carpet."

Nothing short of raging flames or floodwaters would seem important enough to wreck this intimacy, which had materialized like a found treasure in a run-of-the-mill day.

"If the carpet gets ruined, it's my own fault," he murmured, barely finishing the sentence before his mouth met hers. Intense joy welled up as her arms circled his neck and she kissed him back. The pungent scent of paint mingled with the fragrance of her perfume, the blend incredibly enticing and erotic.

Graham was already aroused before he deepened the kiss and mated his tongue passionately with hers. There was no conscious thought of where fondling would lead as he tugged her T-shirt free of her jeans and slipped his hand underneath. Her skin was warm and satin smooth. He caressed a path to her breasts and claimed each one in turn, taking male delight in their shape and firmness, encased in silky nylon and lace.

Holly reacted by arching her back with her own delight when he easily located her hardened peaks and pinched them gently.

The muffled sound in her throat seemed like some kind of signal, giving him greater liberties.

Graham slid his hand around to her back and undid her bra. It was a totally useless garment, he confirmed, capturing a bare breast that didn't need uplifting or support. But it needed to be kissed. Tasted.

Holly was obviously on the same wavelength. She tore her lips apart from his and helped him pull up her T-shirt and strip it over her head along with the bra. Now she was naked from the waist up. Graham had to take a few seconds and admire her luscious beauty even though the tempo of sensual gratification had quickened, taken on more urgency.

"Yes," she whispered, bliss in her voice when he bent his head and pleasured her with his mouth and tongue. "That feels incredibly *good...*"

But Holly didn't remain passive long, a fact that didn't bode well for Graham's control. She tugged his shirttails free and stroked his back with her palms, then raked his skin with her nails. Shudders of passion rippled through Graham. His blood was racing through his veins, sending out heat in waves.

You should stop now if you're going to stop, a voice told him. About that time Holly moved her hips in a writhing motion. The next thing Graham knew he was unzipping her jeans and thrusting his hand inside her silk bikini panties. Any remaining restraint was destroyed when she parted her thighs, allowing him free access.

Desire took over every compartment of Graham's

brain once he'd delved into the lavalike proof of her sexual need. For him.

The tempo kicked into a frenzied pace as though the earth had started spinning faster around its axis. Place didn't matter. Comfort didn't factor in as important. Shedding clothes as fast as possible took the highest priority. Once they were naked, the whole universe consisted of touching, kissing, hugging, stroking. Language was restricted to murmured words of passion and groans and sighs.

Then Holly spoke in a tone of desperation. "You do know this is me, Holly? Not Heather?"

The words acted like ice water raining down on Graham's desire-inflamed body and restoring his faculty of reason. He sat up, shocked at himself and disgusted with his behavior. The same kind of behavior that had allowed Heather to use him to father the twins. Shouldn't he have learned the importance of keeping his cool with all women, for Pete's sake?

Holly sat up, too, with her back to him. "Whatever you say, don't apologize," she said. "If you do, I'll slap you." She sounded on the verge of tears.

"There wasn't ever any doubt who I was kissing and touching just now," he replied, wanting badly to take her into his arms. But he didn't dare.

"Yeah. Sure. That's why you stopped cold when I brought up her name."

"I didn't give Heather a thought, Holly. That's

the problem. I should keep her in the forefront of my mind. The last thing I need is to get hung up on you.''

''Because you're still convinced I'm like her, I suppose.''

''Because I don't trust myself to figure out *who* you really are. It's pretty damn obvious I'm blind where women are concerned.''

''I'm exactly who and what I seem to be on the surface.''

''A career woman who isn't interested in ever getting married and having a family. Right?''

She sighed and reached for her bra. ''I'd love to have a career and a family, Graham, if I believed I could have both. But I don't. And divorce is just too devastating.''

''You're not willing to gamble on marriage, even though there are some lasting marriages.''

''When I spoke wedding vows, I would mean them in my heart. The idea of entrusting my happiness to someone else, of being that vulnerable— well, it scares me to death. Time and time I've seen the same thing happen. Two people who are crazy about each other, who can't get enough of being together, end up as enemies. It's too horrible, and it's not for me.'' She was slipping her arms into her stretchy T-shirt.

''Great. Just great,'' Graham muttered, snatching up his underwear.

They got dressed in silence. The faint sound of music coming from the headphones got on Graham's nerves, and he found the paint odor repugnant.

"I'm sorry," Holly said. She seemed as down in the dumps as he was. "I truly am. You make me wish I could be more optimistic about marriage."

"Why is that? You like guys who're saps?" Graham fell back on bitterness as badly needed protection.

"Don't put yourself down. You're a wonderful man."

"Sure."

"You are!" She took a step toward him, hand outstretched to touch him. Abruptly she stopped and dropped her arm. "Darn!" she murmured in frustration.

The conversation had reached a dead end.

Graham remembered the dropped paint container. He looked around and located it, seeing that pale yellow paint formed a thick pool on the drop cloth. On the way over to the spot, he scooped up a rag.

"Let me mop that up," Holly said. "You might get paint on your nice clothes." She took the rag from his hand.

Rather than stand there and watch her, he rescued the paintbrush. Then needing to focus on something besides what had just happened, he studied the penciled outline of the mural she'd drawn on the wall before she'd begun painting.

"We're in luck," Holly said. "This canvas drop cloth did its job. Your carpet isn't stained."

Graham made some appropriate reply, keeping his thoughts to himself. He would gladly have taken a ruined carpet in exchange for a totally different outcome. It wasn't just the interrupted sex that had left him feeling so dissatisfied. The talk afterward had depressed the hell out of him.

Chapter Nine

''**B**renda Fuselier is on the phone, Graham. Jennifer is running a fever and has thrown up.'' Angela spoke from the door of Graham's office. She screened all his calls during the morning, his most creative part of the day when he concentrated on design work.

Graham got up at once from his drawing table, and took the call. Brenda Fuselier was the director of the preschool in which he'd enrolled Jennifer and Justin. All concern, he listened attentively to her more-detailed description of events concerning his daughter's sudden illness.

''She seemed fine when I dropped them off,'' he

said, vague guilt gnawing at him. Maybe he'd missed some telltale symptoms an experienced parent would have noticed.

"It's probably a virus. You'll need to come and get her right away and take her to her pediatrician."

"I'll be there right away."

Fortunately, Holly had brought up the subject of a pediatrician, and Graham had already set up a well-child appointment for the twins with Dr. Brad Lovett, who had a thriving pediatric practice in partnership with two other children's specialists. Otherwise Graham might have been even less prepared for a medical emergency. He quickly phoned the doctor now to let him know he was bringing his daughter in.

Twenty minutes later he parked his car at the preschool and hurried inside. The sight of Jennifer, wan and yet flushed, did nothing to ease his worried state of mind. Graham squatted down and gently placed his palm against her small forehead. She was unnaturally hot to the touch.

What if this was something more than a virus? he thought, hit by a wave of alarm. What if his little daughter had contracted a serious childhood disease?

"I don't feel good," she complained listlessly.

"Your daddy's taking you to see a doctor, sweetie," Brenda said in a kind tone. "You can go with him now."

Graham stood up and reached for Jennifer's hand. It felt hot, too. "You want me to carry you, baby?" he asked.

To his surprise, she nodded. When he picked her up, she put her arms around his neck and lay her head on his shoulder. Graham hugged her limp, feverish body and spoke words of reassurance, trying to sound confident, "Dr. Lovett will know what to do to make you feel better, baby."

"Dr. Lovett's a very good pediatrician," Brenda said, patting Graham on the arm as she ushered him out. He realized she was reassuring him as much as she was reassuring Jennifer.

The doctor's waiting room was filled with mothers and children of various ages, ranging from infants to preteens. Graham was the only father with a sick child. He took the single remaining chair and sat, cradling Jennifer on his lap.

"You know they're ill when they don't show any interest in the toys," commented a woman who was holding her daughter on her lap, too.

The remark did nothing to ease Graham's parental anxiety.

"Look, Jennifer. Holly's van is parked in our driveway." Graham leaned into the back seat of his car to unbuckle his daughter's seat belt.

She opened her eyes, but showed none of the

enthusiasm she would normally have shown at the prospect of seeing Holly.

"Let's get you inside and start you on this medicine Dr. Lovett prescribed." The session with the pediatrician had allayed the worst of Graham's fears about Jennifer's long-term health. Dr. Lovett's diagnosis had confirmed Brenda Fuselier's. Jennifer had contracted a virus.

"Is it nasty medicine?" the little girl asked.

"The pharmacist said it's cherry-flavored."

He lifted her out, thinking not for the first time today, This car has to go. It wasn't a family automobile, which was what he needed now.

"Hi. How is Jennifer?" Holly called, emerging from his condo. "I phoned your office earlier and Angela told me you'd taken her to the doctor."

Evidently Holly had been keeping a watch out for them, Graham surmised. "You might want to keep your distance from us," he cautioned. "She has a virus."

Holly ignored the warning. She met him halfway and then changed directions, accompanying him back toward the front door. "Poor darling. Do you feel bad?" she asked his daughter who, much to Graham's surprise, hadn't reached out her arms to Holly.

Jennifer nodded. "But my daddy got me medicine from the pharmacy to make me well."

Graham couldn't quite believe he'd heard right. Holly met his gaze, her expression tender.

"Your daddy takes good care of you and Justin, doesn't he, precious?"

"Uh-huh."

Graham had never experienced quite the same humble emotion. His daughter's vote of confidence meant a great deal to him. He had a long way to go before he would consider himself a good father, but becoming one suddenly seemed a reward in itself.

And the effort more voluntary, coming from the heart, not just his conscience.

"You have my car phone number and beeper number. I won't be more than twenty or twenty-five minutes away."

"If I get alarmed, I'll definitely call you," Holly assured Graham. She'd accompanied him downstairs, and he was about to leave.

It had been her suggestion that he return to work and leave Jennifer in her care. Holly planned to devote the afternoon to painting the murals, anyway. She could look in on the little girl often. Right now Jennifer was fast asleep in the master bedroom, where Graham had tucked her in gently after first giving her a dose of medicine in liquid form.

Standing nearby and watching father attend to

small daughter had caused a lump to come to Holly's throat.

"By the way, did you try to get me at my office earlier today for any particular reason?" he asked.

Holly considered fibbing. But fibs were really lies. "Actually, I called to back out on Sunday."

"Because of what happened between us yesterday?"

"Yes. I figured you were probably having second thoughts, too, and were wishing you hadn't invited me to your parents' home."

"You don't want to go?"

Holly stuck with the complicated truth. "Not *wanting* to go had nothing to do with backing out. It's just that you're wasting your time with me."

"Because you're dead set against marriage, you mean."

"Right. And you would do better to put your energy into a relationship that would pan out."

He nodded as though he had no trouble grasping her point, nor did he disagree with her. Holly felt an illogical stab of hurt that he hadn't disagreed. "For the record, I don't regret inviting you," he said. "And I hope you will still come along, if Jennifer is well by Sunday. If she isn't, I'll have to cancel."

"And Justin may get sick with the same virus in the meanwhile."

"The chances are more than fifty-fifty. It won't

surprise me if I get another call from the preschool before the day is over.''

"Enough conversation.'' Holly shooed him toward the door, ridiculously cheerful in the face of the daunting prospect of two sick children. A let's-deal-with-the-present urgency took away the pressure of weighing future actions. "We'd both better get back to work and accomplish as much as we can.''

"Thanks a million. Words that are becoming my theme song.'' He clasped her shoulders and kissed her on the mouth. A brief, firm kiss that flooded her with warmth and light.

"Bye," she said, finally trusting her voice as he was disappearing through the front door.

Long after she'd gone back upstairs, checked on Jennifer and resumed her painting, Holly felt the strong, gentle grip of Graham's hands on her shoulders, the pressure of his mouth on hers. Also, the sense of happiness remained. Holly wielded her artist's brush with an inspired pleasure.

And with love.

This job had been a labor of love, right from the start, she acknowledged to herself. That's why it was so different, so rewarding. The twins had walked right into Holly's heart. So had their dad.

"Was that my daddy on the phone?'' Jennifer asked weakly after Holly had finished her conversation with Graham.

"Yes, sweetie. He's bringing Justin home from preschool. Your brother is sick, too."

"Did Justin go to the doctor?"

"No, your daddy checked with Dr. Lovett. Since the symptoms are the same, Dr. Lovett put Justin on the medicine you're taking." Holly had just given Jennifer a dose when the phone had rung. "Let's put a clean nightie on you. Okay?" The little girl had sweated off her fever, and her nightgown was damp with perspiration.

"Okay."

After Holly had made her small patient comfortable again, she gathered up the discarded nightgown and the clothes Jennifer had worn to preschool and was descending the stairs when Graham entered the condo, carrying a pale Justin.

The little boy lifted his head in response to Holly's sympathetic greeting. "I vomited in Daddy's car," he said, obviously upset with himself. Upset enough in his ill state that he'd referred to his father as Daddy without self-consciousness. Holly was touched as she'd been earlier when the words *my daddy* had come naturally from Jennifer, signaling the crumbling of her resistance to Graham's paternity.

Bonding was taking place, slowly but surely. Holly felt highly privileged to share the growth of the father-child relationship, a process as beautiful as the gradual unfolding of a flower or leaf.

"It's not a big deal, son," Graham was chiding Justin. The word *son* slipped out without any awkwardness. "Like I told you, the car can be cleaned. Let's get you upstairs and into your pajamas."

"I'll be up in a minute to collect his clothes," Holly said, continuing to the laundry room. Graham could handle the situation fine on his own now, whereas just a couple of days ago he could have used her assistance.

By the time she went back upstairs, there was more laundry to be done. Justin had upchucked on the bedsheets.

Changing the sheets and settling the twins back in bed was a job more easily accomplished by two people. Holly was glad she was there to pitch in and help. She wouldn't have wanted to be anywhere else in the whole world.

"How will you manage tonight?" Holly handed Graham her supper plate for him to place it in the dishwasher. He'd made a quick trip to a Chinese restaurant and bought take-out. They'd eaten, pausing between bites to listen in case Justin or Jennifer called out from upstairs.

"I'll just have to catch some sleep sitting in the chair in my bedroom," he replied. Obviously he'd already given the matter some thought.

"You won't get much rest sitting in a chair all

night. You'll be dead tomorrow.'' She carried their empty water glasses over to him.

"The first couple of nights after I brought the kids home with me, I just slept in snatches on the sofa. I got up every hour or two and checked on them. And I survived.''

"You looked pretty haggard,'' Holly recalled. "Plus the twins were healthy and didn't require nursing care. Why don't I spend the night, and we'll take shifts?''

Graham closed the dishwasher door. "Thanks for offering, but you've already done a lot. You took care of Jennifer this afternoon, played nurse tonight, plus washed a couple of loads of laundry.''

"I insist,'' she stated, prepared to dig in and be stubborn.

He was about to answer when he cocked his head. "Did you hear something?''

They both listened and heard faint childish voices.

"I'll go,'' he said.

"I'll go with you.''

Mounting the stairs side by side, they could make out the words summoning them. "Daddy. Holly.''

"They've both started calling you Daddy,'' Holly commented.

"And you know what's strange?'' He sounded half-sheepish, half-awed. "I like it.''

The admission touched Holly deep in her heart. "Watch out. They'll be wrapping Daddy around their little pinkies."

"I can see the danger of that happening," Graham said ruefully. "For the first time, I understand why parents might have trouble being disciplinarians. Before, I was always critical."

"You'll be too good a daddy to let Justin and Jennifer run wild and become brats." Holly hooked her arm in his.

"Thanks," he said, hugging her arm tightly against his side.

Outside the master bedroom, he paused long enough to give her a bear hug and a kiss very much like his goodbye kiss earlier in the afternoon, only slightly more lingering. The effect was the same, switching on warmth and light. And happiness.

"Graham. Wake up," Holly whispered. Gently she patted his cheek.

He opened his eyes wide, coming alert.

"It's your turn to sleep on the sofa," she explained in a whisper. His gaze was going over her in the dim light of the master bedroom. Holly knew she looked anything but alluring in his size extra-large T-shirt she was wearing as a nightgown, but she suddenly felt alluring. He definitely was sexy in his boxer shorts, his chest and shoulders bare.

"I'm fine here. You keep the sofa," he said.

"That wasn't our deal. Up." She grasped his hands and tugged. Instead of rising, he tugged back and pulled her onto his lap.

"Graham." She murmured his name in protest. Very weak protest. He was hugging her tight, and it felt wonderful to cuddle against him. The twins were sleeping soundly, evidently resting well and not needing attention for the moment. Holly had touched her palm to their foreheads before waking Graham, and had determined that they didn't seem feverish.

"I was dreaming about you," Graham said, his voice a caress.

"A nice dream?"

"Very nice."

"I'm glad it wasn't a nightmare." Holly planted a tender kiss on his hard jaw, another on his cheek. With an audible intake of breath, he turned his head toward her, offering access to his mouth. She bumped her nose against his before she kissed him on the lips.

He kissed her back, and they traded short, loving kisses until their lips started to cling. Holly's mouth parted and her tongue played with his, the delicious intimacy extending to tasting. Graham stroked her legs, adding another dimension to her pleasure. His hand slid under the T-shirt and found sensitive, bare skin.

"You're turning me on," Holly whispered with

regret. She hated to call a halt, especially since he was already aroused. She could feel his erection pressing again her hip.

"I want you so much," he said, his voice full of longing. But he withdrew his hand and caressed her back and shoulders with the T-shirt acting as a barrier.

Holly kneaded his shoulders lovingly, raining kisses on his face. She'd never dealt with this tender urge to satisfy a man and make him happy. Sex had always been more of a selfish act somehow. "We could go downstairs and make love on the sofa."

"Don't tempt me, darling." He hugged her tightly. "I can wait. When I make love with you, I don't want it to be a quickie on the sofa. We'd both have one ear trained in case one of the kids woke up and cried out."

"Next week we should be moving them into their bedroom." The *we* had slipped out.

"That's good."

Holly rested her cheek against his. "Just 'good'? Won't you be thrilled to get your bedroom back?"

"Sure. But I'd keep sleeping on the sofa if it meant keeping you around longer. I like seeing you every day."

"I like seeing you every day, too."

He seemed content to leave the conversation there.

Holly would have expected to be relieved he

didn't have more to say on the subject of a continuing relationship. Instead she felt a nagging dissatisfaction.

What's your problem? she asked herself after Graham had surrendered the chair to her and gone downstairs at her prodding. You don't want him to say he's falling in love with you, do you?

To Holly's confusion and dismay, the answer from within her wasn't a resounding *no*.

It was one thing for her to buy into heartache by getting too fond of Graham. But she wouldn't cause him heartache for the world.

"Shhh. Holly's sleeping in the chair."

"She stayed here all night?"

Holly awoke to childish voices. Opening her eyes, she saw Jennifer and Justin peering at her from the bed, looking remarkably as though they'd been restored to good health.

"Boo!" she said playfully, and they giggled in response.

Evidently they construed her waking up as an invitation because both of them slid to the floor and trotted over to climb up in her lap. She circled each small body and they hugged her around the neck. When she kissed them on the cheek, they each gave her a sweet kiss in return.

"What a way to start off the day, with a hug and a kiss!" Holly said.

"Where's Daddy?" Justin asked.

"Downstairs on the sofa."

"No, he isn't," Graham said, entering, wearing nothing but his boxer shorts. He yawned and smiled at the three of them. "Looks like the medicine did the trick," he commented to Holly.

"Isn't it miraculous?"

"I'll say. I want to buy some stock in that pharmaceutical company."

"Holly stayed here all night, Daddy!" Jennifer exclaimed.

"She slept in the chair," Justin elaborated.

"Not all night. Your daddy slept here part of the time while I had the sofa," Holly put in. Silently she amended the sentence to "Your sexy daddy." He was definitely a hunk with his dark hair rumpled and the majority of his fit, athletic body exposed to view. A lovable hunk. Holly felt an overwhelming urge to hug him and kiss him, too.

Graham seemed to respond to her need for affectionate contact, or else he acted to satisfy his own urge. He walked over close and used both hands to ruffle Justin's and Jennifer's hair. Then he smoothed back Holly's hair, leaned down and kissed her on the cheek. Still bent over, he gave each of his children a kiss, too.

Some instinct told Holly she was witnessing the first time he'd kissed them. "Now, how about a hug?'' she said, her chest swelled with happy emotion.

He squatted down and slipped his arms around all three of them.

Justin and Jennifer giggled delightedly. Holly took advantage of the wonderful proximity and pressed a kiss to his stubbled cheek. The twins followed her example, with Jennifer exclaiming, ''Daddy's cheek is scratchy!''

''Wait until I've shaved, and it'll be smooth,'' Graham said.

''Can we watch?'' Justin asked.

Holly had trouble restraining a grin at Graham's expression. He looked totally nonplussed at the unexpected request. ''Your daddy probably wants privacy in the bathroom this morning,'' she said, coming to his rescue. ''While he's taking his shower and shaving, we can get dressed and go downstairs to the kitchen and fix some breakfast.''

Graham overruled that plan, sending Holly off to take her shower first while he helped the twins get dressed. Holly didn't argue. A shower sounded too good.

With the warm spray pelting her body, she hummed one of her many favorite classic rock tunes and felt as if she were brimming over with happiness. Waking up alone at her house was never this much fun.

This morning was like a preview of what life

could be like if she and Graham were man and wife, and the four of them made up a family. The thought was so incredibly appealing, it brought a goofy smile to Holly's face.

The smile became wistful as she gave herself a reality check. Marriages don't last and families break up regularly, Holly. Remember that. Do I have to? she asked herself. Yes, if you're smart you'll imagine a preview of what divorcing Graham would be like in five years or ten years.

Holly postponed any further soul searching. After all, she was jumping the gun. She and Graham hadn't even dated, for heaven's sake. They hadn't slept together. If and when they did—probably *when* rather than *if*—the sizzle of attraction might die down. Their relationship might never go beyond friendship. The issue of marriage might never arise.

Eventually Graham would marry someone. Holly didn't pursue that line of thought, either. It was much too depressing.

Chapter Ten

"I'm glad you called and suggested lunch on the spur of the moment." Patricia was opening up her menu as she spoke. "I had a million and one things to do and didn't feel like doing any of them."

"Same here," Holly said.

"You?" The other woman raised her eyebrows in surprise. "My excuse is divorce apathy. What's yours?"

Holly made a face. "I guess I'm miffed because I have my Saturday free."

"How did you hope to be occupied?"

"If I explain, I'll sound like a nitwit who doesn't know her own mind."

Patricia gestured as though to say, "So?"

"To fill you in on some background, last week I spent a great deal of time at Graham Knight's condo. He won the free decorating prize at the raffle."

"Right. He's a local architect. You're doing a bedroom for his twins he suddenly got custody of. Five-year-olds?"

"They're three and a half. A girl and boy. And adorable. I've gotten very fond of them. And very fond of Graham. By Friday night, though, I'd decided I needed some breathing space and I wouldn't see them today. Graham must have decided the same thing."

"Oh. So he didn't make any plans and include you."

Holly shook her head glumly.

"Hmmm. You say you're 'fond' of him. Just how fond?"

"I've never liked a guy this much, never wanted to be *with* a guy this much. I got up this morning and I missed him. Missed the kids," Holly added.

"Uh-oh. Sounds like you've got a bad case." Patricia sighed and her expression reflected sadness. "I envy you. There's nothing quite like falling in love."

"You're in the process of getting a divorce, and you *envy* me?"

"Just because my relationship with Roger went sour, that doesn't mean yours would."

"It probably would, and I couldn't stand that."

Their waitress came, and they ordered. After she'd gone, Patricia continued the conversation as though there had been no interruption. "I still think you're being too pessimistic. But there's an added risk you need to factor in. You've already become attached to those children, and you'd be a stepmother if you married Graham, not a birth mother with grounds for partial custody if you ever divorced."

"Graham would be fair," Holly protested.

"Don't be so sure," Patricia said, her tone cynical. "I would never have dreamed Roger was capable of being as petty as he has turned out to be. Did I tell you the nervy bastard wants the value of the jewelry he bought me figured into our estate? And he wants the Rockford crystal! Can you believe his gall when *he* screwed around, not me?"

"Unfortunately, I can." Roger's behavior wasn't atypical of men divorcing their wives. It dawned on Holly that she'd sought out Patricia's company partly because of the need for a reminder of the bleak facts of life about couples and marriage and divorce.

Love turned sour over time. Tenderness and caring died. Marriages failed. People who'd been devoted to each other haggled over possessions.

Holly would be selling herself a false bill of goods if she bought in to the hope that she and Graham could beat the enormous odds.

They couldn't.

And it was just too darned bad. The single life had never before seemed lonely as it did now.

After lunch she forced herself to run a few errands and then went home and made phone calls to clients, looked through catalogs and, in general, focused attention on several jobs in progress that she'd put on a back burner this past week.

Every time she answered an incoming call, her heart leaped with eagerness at the possibility that Graham might be phoning her. Every time it was someone else's voice, her heart sank with disappointment. You're acting like a lovesick idiot, Holly, she berated herself.

One of the callers turned out to be her mother, Elaine, who'd started out life as Elaine Vickers and since then become Elaine Beaumont, Elaine Ellington, Elaine Wade. Currently her surname was Holmes.

"Hi, honey," she greeted her daughter and only child. "I wanted to catch you early before you went out."

"I hope you aren't sitting home tonight, Mother," Holly teased, knowing her mother was fitting the call into her busy social schedule.

Elaine laughed. "No, Lyle and I are going to a

dinner party. It'll probably be deadly dull. The guests are all college professors and spouses or significant others.'' Lyle Holmes was a biology professor at LSU in Baton Rouge, the capital city of Louisiana and about an hour's drive from the North Shore.

"I thought you found it very stimulating to be around academics."

"I did—er, I do. Too much of any good thing gets old, don't you agree?"

Holly groaned. "Don't tell me you're getting dissatisfied with Husband Number Four, Mother."

"Don't fret, Holly. Lyle and I are still lovey-dovey when we're alone together. So how's your love life? Have you started dating anyone?"

"Not exactly. But there is a guy I like a lot." She told her mother about Graham.

Elaine's enthusiasm cooled with the mention of the twins. "Date him and have fun, but don't get serious," she cautioned.

"Why not?"

"I see problems with taking on an instant family. You would miss out on a honeymoon. And that's the most wonderful stage of marriage." Elaine chuckled. "I should know, honey."

Belatedly Holly realized she hadn't reiterated her stand that she never intended marrying. Her mother had always brushed it aside anyway, telling Holly she would eventually fall in love and take the plunge.

"But I enjoy those times when I'm around Graham and his children, just like I enjoy the two of us being alone. He's so gentle with them. Being a father brings out such fine qualities in his character."

"All men have fine qualities. They all have not-so-fine qualities that can come out later, too," Elaine stated. "Holly, don't even *consider* marrying this architect-father without a prenuptial contract. One that gives you custody rights to those darling children if and when you split up with their daddy."

It seemed uncanny that two people today had given Holly this same advice.

"Mother, I hate the very idea of a prenuptial contract! It goes contrary to the marriage vows."

"Do it for me. When you become a stepmother, you'll be making me a grandmother. And I won't have a legal leg to stand on."

"Graham isn't the type of person—" Holly broke off her protest. It wouldn't carry any more weight with her mother than it had with Patricia. "This whole discussion is premature. I may never have to decide whether or not to marry Graham."

"That might be the best scenario."

Elaine changed the subject and they chatted another fifteen minutes. Holly had trouble carrying her end of the conversation because her mind was so troubled.

Did Graham have a visitor? Holly wondered, eyeing a brand-new minivan parked in his driveway. It still had a temporary license plate from the dealer.

Instead of using her key, Holly pressed the doorbell button. Almost immediately the door swung open, and Justin and Jennifer flung themselves at her, shouting her name in excited greeting.

"Holly! Holly!"

Graham stood in the open doorway, incredibly handsome in khaki slacks and a striped cotton shirt. His smile welcomed her arrival.

All the unhappy emotion that had built up the previous day evaporated in the pure gladness of being reunited with the three of them. Reunited? After a day's separation? Holly dismissed analysis and hugged and kissed the twins, receiving hugs and kisses in return.

"Hi," Graham greeted her when she'd entered the foyer.

"Hi." She smiled back at him.

"What about me?" he asked. "Don't I rate a kiss?"

"You sure do." Holly stepped close and raised up on tiptoe to give him a peck on the cheek. He angled his head so that their lips met. Immediately his arms came around her, enclosing her in a sensory heaven. Holly breathed in the scent of his soap and aftershave and reveled in the brief intimacy of pressing her body against his.

"I missed you yesterday," he told her, his voice another pleasure.

"I missed you, too."

Justin and Jennifer were clamoring for attention, demanding to know, "Are we going now, Daddy? Holly's here."

Graham squeezed her tighter before he released her. "Yes, we're going right away."

"Whose blue minivan in the driveway?" Holly asked.

"It's my daddy's," Justin answered.

"Yours?" She looked questioningly at Graham, who nodded.

"I did most of my shopping by phone yesterday," he said. "Making the rounds of the dealers wasn't feasible with two small kids."

Holly bit her lip to keep from saying she would have liked to go automobile shopping with him. It would have been a fun outing and she could have helped keep a rein on the twins. Instead he'd managed on his own and excluded her.

"I traded in my truck," he was explaining. "But I plan to get rid of the car, too. I know a guy who wants to buy it."

"Gosh, I didn't realize you were even considering buying a minivan.'' He hadn't mentioned a word about his intentions.

Did he buy and sell automobiles on a whim? Or had he been mulling the idea over all week and simply not been inclined to run it by her and get her opinion?

It shook Holly that she could be taken so off guard by Graham. I don't really know him well at all, she thought. And yet yesterday she'd risen to his defense twice, ready to argue about how he would behave in a divorce situation.

The four of them trooped out to the new minivan. Graham opened the front passenger door for Holly and slid open the side door for the twins to scramble up onto the middle bench seat. He played referee when they squabbled over who would sit by the window on the bench seat. Just a week ago, he'd stood by helplessly, Holly recalled.

''Anything wrong?'' Graham asked when he'd gotten behind the wheel.

''Why do you ask?'' she answered, evading a yes or no.

''You're kind of low-key today.'' He started the engine, his gaze still searching her face. ''The color? You don't like this shade of blue?''

''No. I do like it. I guess I was just taken aback to find a brand-new automobile sitting in your driveway. I probably figured I was the impulsive one between the two of us.''

He shifted into reverse and started backing out. "Normally I'm not impulsive about major purchases except for automobiles. I bought my truck and my car each in a single weekend."

"So you woke up yesterday morning and the urge to buy a minivan hit you?"

He grinned. "An ad in the newspaper reached out and grabbed me."

Holly suddenly felt a hundred percent more cheerful that he hadn't been secretive, after all. "I love this new-car smell," she said.

The hour-and-a-half drive, part of which was interstate travel, didn't seem nearly that long. The terrain had changed from flat to gentle rolling hills when Graham turned off a two-lane rural Mississippi highway onto a gravel driveway. Holly admired the charming entrance, which was planted with shrubs and flowers.

The driveway wound through woods and then was flanked by fenced pastures. Justin and Jennifer bounced up and down on their seats with excitement, spotting half a dozen grazing horses, two of which were colts. The sprawling one-story brick house was located on a hill overlooking a small lake with a dock and a rowboat. In the background, a barn and several outbuildings, all neatly painted barn red, completed the picture.

"What a great place for Grandma and Grandpa

to live and their grandchildren to visit!'' Holly exclaimed, entranced.

"Speaking of Grandma and Grandpa," Graham said, killing the engine.

His parents, a spry couple in their fifties, had emerged from the house, all smiles. The smiles went slack, almost wiped out by surprise, when Holly stepped out into view. Is it my outfit? Holly wondered, a vision of her walk-in closet littered with discarded garments flashing before her eyes. She hadn't been so undecided over what to wear since she was a teenager, finally selecting a calf-length gathered skirt in a paisley print, a simple white blouse and flats. The keynotes were feminine, comfortable and not too casual.

No, her outfit was fine. The truth hit Holly. Valerie and Gerald Knight must have met Heather and apparently remembered her well enough that they saw a marked resemblance between Graham's old flame and Holly.

Darn it! Holly muttered silently in dismay. She wished she'd looked like *anybody* else!

"Why don't you show Holly those samples of cloth for the new living room drapes, Val? Maybe she could help you decide."

Gerald offered this suggestion following the marvelous Sunday dinner that had been spoiled for Holly because nearly every time she'd spoken, she'd gotten the impression she might as well be reciting dialogue from a play that Graham's parents had attended. They'd sneaked glances at each other that had said plainly, *We've heard this before, haven't we?*

Holly's conversational offerings had been social chitchat, remarks like ''Val, you're a marvelous cook. Graham didn't brag about you enough.'' And ''What a lovely view of the lake from your dining room window!'' If Graham had brought Heather here to visit, no doubt she might have said the same things almost verbatim.

No *if* about it. Heather *had* been here first.

''I'd love to look at those fabric samples,'' Holly said, trying hard not to let the situation bug her. The important issue here was grandparents getting acquainted with new grandchildren, and that part of the day was going great. Jennifer and Justin were fast recovering from their shyness and responding to the doting attention of Grandma and Grandpa Knight.

''You and Mom, come outside and join us at the lake when you're finished,'' Graham said to Holly. The plan was for Gerald to take the twins for a ride in the rowboat. Later Val would introduce them to her horses, for she was the horse trainer, not her husband.

Holly managed not to give Graham a reproachful look before she followed after his pint-size, energetic mother. Later, Holly would rake Graham over the coals for not mentioning he'd brought Heather to meet his parents. Holly might have been more prepared for her reception.

"I hate this decorating stuff," Val declared, pulling swatches out of a drawer in the living room. "I'm just not good at it."

"Your home is very inviting," Holly said, phrasing her compliment to be truthful. Instantly she sensed that Val had been treated to the same tact before. By Heather, no doubt. "Val, could we be very open?" Holly blurted.

The other woman blinked. "Sure."

"You and Gerald must have met Heather Booth when Graham was dating her. You both find it disconcerting that I look like her, don't you?"

"Very disconcerting. When you got out of the minivan, I thought for a second, 'Am I seeing a ghost? Didn't Graham say Heather had been killed?'" Val went on. "He brought her here one weekend. My older son, Greg, was visiting from Houston with his daughter, Bridget, who was four then. Gerald took a whole roll of film that day."

"He snapped some pictures of Graham and Heather. And you looked at them again recently," Holly guessed aloud.

"Yes."

"Could I see those pictures?"

Val got a photo album and flipped through the

pages before handing the album to Holly. "Good-ness," Holly murmured, gazing at a pretty blond woman dressed in a calf-length skirt, simple blouse and flats. "There is a resemblance."

"I hope it's only outward. What she did was wrong. And to think she was carrying out her scheme the whole time she was a guest in our home." Val shook her head, indignant as well as disapproving. "Graham hasn't brought anybody else here since. I got the impression he wasn't dat-ing much the last four years or so, after he broke off with Heather. It's pretty obvious he likes you a lot...." Her voice drifted off. "As a mother, I find it odd, you know?"

"I don't have any kind of scheme," Holly stated. She handed Val the album and picked up the swatches of material, focusing upon them with an effort. "Which of these do you like best?"

"Actually none of them. They're all blah, but I figured I was better off being safe."

Blah was the right word, but Holly diplomati-cally didn't say so. "Why don't I pick out several not-so-safe fabrics I think would look good and send you swatches?"

The other woman brightened. "I'll take you up on that offer."

They went outside to join the men and children. But Holly found it impossible to relax and enjoy herself. She kept seeing the photos of Heather

Booth, one in particular with Graham's arm around her. Val Knight's troubled words kept playing in her head. *As a mother, I find it odd, you know?*

How do you think I feel? Holly thought unhappily.

"Graham, Justin and Jennifer are precious."

"They're cute kids, if I do say so myself." Graham smiled sheepishly at his mother, who'd pulled him aside. "Do I sound like a proud father or what?"

"You're going to make a good father, and I couldn't be prouder of you."

"Thanks, Mom. I'm trying hard. Holly's been a major help. I don't know how I would have gotten though last week without her."

Val's smile faded. "Be careful, son. I don't want to see you get hurt again."

"Mom, Holly isn't Heather. She's honest and upfront." Warm. Generous. Caring. Graham listed more attributes silently that he'd never associated with his children's mother.

"Still, take your time and get to know her well," his mother urged.

"Don't you like her?"

"I liked Heather. So what kind of judge of character does that make me?"

The same kind of judge of character I am, Graham thought.

His mother was still talking. "I see red every time I think about her coming here and being friendly while all the time she was planning to have my grandbaby and never let me see it. Never let me know it existed!"

"Holly wouldn't do anything like that, Mom."

"Take your time and get to know her before you decide what kind of person she is, Graham. Please."

Then Val hooked her arm in his, and changed the subject to a lighter one. "Ready for a second helping of my homemade blueberry pie?"

Graham didn't much relish the second round of dessert. His mother's advice seemed to have destroyed his taste buds. It was good advice, and the conversation with her reawakened his cautiousness about trusting Holly.

The twins had missed their afternoon nap and were irritable for the first fifteen minutes of the return trip home. Then suddenly they both fell to sleep, right in the middle of a quarrel.

Tenderness welled up in Holly as she glanced back and saw that Jennifer was using her Raggedy Ann doll as a pillow and Justin was resting his head on his little sister's shoulder.

"They had such a good day," she said. "Visiting this set of grandparents is like visiting a theme park."

"I'm sorry you didn't have a good day. You didn't, did you?" His gaze held apology.

"How could I?" Holly's indignation found voice in words. "Graham, why the devil didn't you prepare Gerald and Val for meeting me? Why didn't you prepare me for meeting them? It didn't even occur to me that they'd gotten to know Heather and would react the same way you did when you met me."

"They were around her just one day, and I had halfway forgotten bringing her to Picayune."

"Your mother has pictures of Heather in an album! She showed them to me!"

He muttered a curse. "Why the hell did she do that?"

"I asked to see them. I was curious to find out for myself if there was really a resemblance." Holly sighed. "There was some similarity in looks. Although she was prettier than I am."

"I don't agree."

"I wasn't fishing for a compliment. I was simply stating a fact."

"So was I. Please forgive me for putting you in an awkward situation today. I could have kicked myself."

Kicked himself for bringing her? Holly couldn't find the courage to put that question to him. "Is that why you got more tense as the day went on?"

"Partly." She looked at him inquiringly. He finally continued. "A heart-to-heart talk with my mother made me realize all over again I'm in no mental state to get involved with anyone right now."

"She warned you not to get involved with me, didn't she? Funny, our mothers couldn't be more unlike each other, and they're on the same wavelength. When my mother phoned yesterday, I told her about you, and she advised me not to get involved with a guy with two kids."

"Did you think it was sound advice?" he asked.

"Yes. Depressingly sound advice."

Are you going to take it? Holly waited for him to ask next. When he didn't, the discussion of the pros and cons of a relationship between them seemed to die. Though actually no pros had ever been raised, she reflected, only cons.

Gloom weighed heavy during the remainder of the drive. Rather than make conversation, Holly switched on the radio and thought her own dreary thoughts. She sensed that he was doing the same.

At his condo, she told him and the groggy twins good-night, and he didn't urge her to come in. Obviously he'd decided to take his mother's counsel.

Holly drove home, more down in the dumps than she'd ever been in her adult life. Arriving at her house failed to lift her spirits with a sense of homecoming. Nor did the fast-blinking red light on her answering machine, signaling numerous messages, cheer her up.

None of the voices would be Graham's, a voice she'd come to love.

Chapter Eleven

"Could you move that chest of drawers just a few inches toward the window, please?"

"Like so, ma'am?" The muscular young deliveryman glanced at Holly for her approval.

"That's perfect, Reggie." She replied, reading his name on his uniform.

The other deliveryman, Hank, entered the room, carrying a stack of drawers. After they'd been slid into place, Holly signed a delivery form. Their work completed, the two men paused to look around admiringly at the twins' bedroom.

"This is cool, with scenes painted on the walls like that. And the room divided into a girl half and a boy half. I never seen anything like it,'' Reggie said.

"Me, neither,'' Hank concurred. "It is cool. Well, have a good one.''

They departed, and Holly went into action, making up the two single beds, one with pink-and-white striped sheets and a matching bedspread and the other with sheets and bedspread with a bold blue background and alphabet blocks in primary colors. Justin's mural depicted a scene from his favorite storybook about a toy train, and Jennifer's depicted her favorite story, Snow White and the Seven Dwarfs.

"An adorable room for two adorable children,'' she pronounced in a pleased voice when she'd finished her tasks. "Your best job ever, Holly.''

Not surprising that it was, since she'd put heart and soul into this project. It had taken some doing to complete the job by today, Friday, but she'd met her own deadline.

Coming here to Graham's condo each day had given her a measure of relief from the new loneliness that being around people besides him and the twins didn't seem to alleviate. He hadn't come by to see her. She'd conferred with him on the phone several times, and the exchanges had only left her feeling more emotionally needy.

Was he miserable, too?

Holly sighed. Enough moping. Graham would be

picking up the twins in about an hour. Plenty of time for her to move their things into their bedroom.

Forty-five minutes later she'd finished hanging small garments on children's hangers and placing folded clothing into drawers. She'd also arranged toys and books on shelves.

What now? It wasn't a difficult question to answer. Holly meant to stay here until Justin and Jennifer arrived. She wanted to show them their bedroom herself, show it to Graham, too.

This was quite an event for him as well as the children. Now he could move back into his bedroom after two weeks of sleeping on the sofa, poor guy.

He would probably appreciate having clean sheets, and she had fifteen minutes to kill. Holly headed for the linen closet, acting on her impulse to do something nice for Graham.

"Holly's here, Daddy!"

"That's her minivan, Daddy!"

"I see it," Graham said. He empathized with his children's excitement. He felt damn excited himself at the sight of Holly's vehicle parked at his condo. It seemed more like a month than a week that they'd been avoiding each other, by unspoken agreement.

Graham pulled into the garage, and he and the twins entered through the laundry room door. They ran ahead of him, shouting Holly's name at the top of their lungs.

"Hi, guys!" She greeted the three of them, face alight with gladness.

Jennifer and Justin hurled themselves at her, and she knelt and gathered them close, hugging them. Watching, Graham was filled with yearning. He wished she would hug him tight when his turn came to greet her.

"Your new bedroom's ready. Would you like to go upstairs and take a peek?" Holly asked the twins.

"Will you go upstairs with us?" Justin asked.

"Will you stay and have supper with us?" Jennifer wanted to know.

Obviously neither of them wanted to chance her leaving anytime soon. Graham was completely in agreement with their wish to keep her there.

"I don't know about supper, but I'll stick around a while," Holly promised, and stood up after giving them another hug. Today she wasn't wearing jeans, but was dressed in one of her stylish North-Shore-career-woman outfits.

"Hi," Graham said, finally getting her attention. "How have you been?"

"Busy. How have you been?"

"The same." He knew he was gazing at her hungrily, but he couldn't help himself. It was hell to be this close and not touch her, not kiss her.

"When are we going upstairs?" Jennifer asked impatiently.

Holly broke the eye contact, sucking in a breath. "Right now."

They trooped up the stairs to inspect the bedroom. The twins were entranced with their murals. Graham took as much pleasure in Holly's delight in their appreciative response as he did in their reaction. All week she'd kept the door closed so that Jennifer and Justin would get the full impact of the fanciful scenes when she'd finished painting them. But Graham had observed the evolution. Every night he'd gone into the room after his children were asleep and had admired her artistic talent. Sensing her presence hadn't made him miss her any less. Imagining her at work, paintbrush in hand, certainly hadn't helped him to fall asleep after he'd turned in for the night on the sofa. Still, he'd at least satisfied the craving for her company enough to resist phoning her.

At the moment it seemed a dubious victory of willpower.

"Are you pleased?" she asked Graham while Jennifer and Justin were climbing up on their beds, trying them out.

"More than pleased," he replied. "My kids have the neatest bedroom on the North Shore, thanks to you."

She glowed at his sincere compliment. "I loved doing it."

"You'll have to bill me for the extra week. My raffle prize was Decorator for a Week, not two weeks."

"Don't be silly. Any extra time I spent is my present to Jennifer and Justin."

"How about a barter arrangement? I'll do a free job for you."

"Okay! You can design a gazebo for my backyard. One that will go with my house."

"It's a deal. I'll have to take a look at your house and your backyard. Maybe this weekend."

"Sure. You can bring the twins. We can have a picnic lunch or something."

"Sounds good."

Better than good. Graham suddenly felt like he had a new lease on life. Dammit, he'd had enough of being cautious and steering clear of Holly because he might fall in love with her. To hell with being wise.

Designing a gazebo for her would give him a legitimate excuse to call her, to see her. Plus he intended to pull out the stops and come up with something really special. Graham wanted to give something of himself, of his talent back to her, like she'd given of herself and her talent to enrich the lives of his children.

A special job for a very special woman.

*   *   *

"Please stay and eat with us, Holly!" Jennifer begged.

"Daddy's making us macaroni and cheese," Justin said, as though offering an inducement.

"If that doesn't stir up your taste buds, I can get us some take-out," Graham said. "Italian. Chinese. Whatever strikes your fancy."

Holly didn't need any more urging to accept the supper invitation. She'd been waiting for some direction from him. "Macaroni and cheese is fine."

Graham groaned. "Oh, come on."

She laughed, amused that he wasn't really clowning. "Why don't I make the macaroni and cheese while you buy take-out of your choice?"

"Best offer I've had all week." He was on his way to the door, walking with springy steps.

Holly got out a saucepan, aware of how happy she felt. To heck with her mother's advice. To heck with his mother's advice. To heck with trying to figure out the future. Right now was what counted. And she couldn't think of any other place she'd rather be, anything else she'd rather be doing.

Graham returned with food from one of Holly's favorite Italian restaurants on the North Shore. He'd bought Caesar salad and fettuccini with spicy crawfish tails and pesto sauce. Holly savored every bite, and it was pretty apparent he did, too.

After supper she helped with the twins' baths and

with getting them into their pajamas. They were too excited over sleeping in their new bedroom to become drowsy right away, but eventually their yawns became frequent and their eyelids drooped. Within seconds of each other, they fell deeply asleep.

Holly kissed each slumbering child on the cheek and so did Graham. He left the door slightly ajar as they were leaving the room.

"That's a good idea. You'll hear them if they call out for you," she whispered.

"Hopefully, one of us will," he said. The husky note in his voice made her heart beat faster.

"I meant after you've gone to bed later. In your own bedroom."

"So did I. I'm hoping—" His arms came around her, and he hugged her tight, letting his embrace complete his sentence. He hoped she would spend the night with him.

Holly hugged him back, content to let actions take the place of discussion. "I missed you so much, Graham."

"I missed you. I can't tell you how hard it was not to come by here during the day."

"I kept wishing you would."

"I knew I wouldn't have the self-control not to kiss you...."

He was kissing her now. Holly framed his face with her hands, answering his urgent need with her own. It was sheer heaven, the warm pressure of his mouth, the intimate coupling of her tongue with his. Holly didn't hold back. She abandoned herself utterly to the pleasure and the escalating passion.

Unexpectedly his arms loosened. *No,* she protested silently, but the next second she was uttering *Yes! Oh, yes...* He'd freed up his hands to caress her body. Every inch of sensitive skin zinged to life under his touch.

They ended the kiss, reaching some wordless accord, not to stop but to pause. Graham picked her up in his arms and carried her into his bedroom.

"I just hope this isn't one of my dreams and I don't wake up, all turned on and no Holly," he said, setting her on her feet.

"It isn't a dream." While they kissed, she unbuttoned his shirt and slipped her hands inside to slide her palms over his chest. His heartbeat thudded beneath the hard-muscled contours furred with soft body hair. Holly reveled in his vitality and manliness, which had attracted her to him from the beginning. Before she'd discovered so many other facets of him to admire. To love.

Without taking his lips from hers, Graham jerked his shirt free of his slacks and shrugged it off, giving Holly the added treat of feeling the smooth play of his muscles. He'd bared his entire upper torso for her to explore. Holly took immediate advantage, glutting herself with pleasure as she stroked his biceps, his shoulders, his taut back.

"You're a gorgeous man," she murmured against his mouth as they both stopped kissing to catch their breath.

"That feels so good for you to touch me."

"Just like your dreams?"

"Better. Much better."

Holly had shed her black linen jacket earlier in the evening and wore the matching skirt and a silk blouse that buttoned partially down her back. Graham undid the buttons, and the two of them removed the blouse. He bent and kissed a trail down to her cleavage while his hands slid bra and slip straps off her shoulders and down her arms. Holly tugged both undergarments down to her waist, exposing her breasts for his enjoyment.

For her enjoyment....

She moaned with the blissful sensations as he nuzzled and kissed and tasted her at his leisure. His low, deep voice and warm breath raised goose bumps when he murmured, "You're so beautiful." Holly felt beautiful. She felt cherished.

At the same time she was aware of being hotly aroused.

Graham raised up as though sensing her urgency or else reacting to his own need. Holly unbuckled his belt, but then he slid down the zipper of his slacks and quickly undressed, leaving her to make short work of shedding the rest of her outfit. Nudity added a whole new dimension of erotic pleasure for Holly. His arousal was magnificently evident.

She reached out and stroked the length of him. He groaned and closed his eyes, but his hands found her breasts and fondled them with a maddening delicacy. Then he slid one hand lower over her stomach, ventured still lower and staked an intimate claim. Holly's hand closed around him in a reflex response to the spasms of desire he'd incited.

"Holly, I want to be inside you, right here," he said, delving into her molten heat.

"No more than I want it."

"Yes, I can tell." His voice was exultant.

He picked her up in his arms and carried her to the bed. Holly waited impatiently while he sheathed himself. She held her arms out to him and drew him to her. He followed her wordless indication of her wishes and positioned himself to join their bodies together. One strong thrust sent him deep inside her. Holly gasped with the ecstatic sensations, arching to take him even deeper.

Graham looked shell-shocked as he gazed into her face. "You're incredible," he said.

"*You're* incredible."

Flooded by tender, jubilant emotion, Holly pulled his head down to kiss him. The kiss was gentle at first, but rapidly grew passionate. Graham set up a slow tempo of lovemaking that quickly went out of control. Holly hung on to him, matching his frenzied rhythm, the two of them riding a roller coaster that went up and up and up with no downward dips.

They zoomed over a peak. Holly cried out with the thrilling joy of her climax, and a second later Graham cried out, too. They'd been ejected from the roller coaster and fortunately had landed on a soft, puffy cloud that drifted down, down, down.

Back to sanity.

Graham slid back into bed and drew Holly into his arms. He nuzzled her hair and spoke with lazy contentment. "That was definitely worth waiting for."

"Yes."

"Right now I'm wondering if I'll ever need sex again."

"Me, too."

She snuggled closer and his satisfaction deepened. He hadn't been this happy and at peace since…when?

Maybe never before? The realization jarred him enough to spoil his complacency. "Will you spend the night?" he asked.

Holly didn't answer at once, and Graham sensed her mental struggle. "I shouldn't," she said finally, regret in her voice.

"Why not?"

"You know why not."

He could guess her reasons, but hearing her spell them out in words was necessary as an antidote to false hopes. "Tell me anyway."

She sighed. "Because I want to, far too much."

"Then stay. We can make love when we wake up in the morning."

"Graham, being sexually compatible doesn't solve all the problems two people face in maintaining a relationship."

"I didn't ask you to get married and live happily ever after. I just invited you to spend the night."

"You have no inkling how much I wish it was possible to marry you and live happily ever after. But it isn't. Otherwise I wouldn't wait for you to propose. I'd ask you to marry me."

"You would?"

"Don't play innocent. That doesn't come as any surprise."

"I'm a guy with a bad track record at reading women's minds, remember."

Holly sat up. "I have to go."

The indirect reference to Heather had put a wedge between them. Graham realized he'd spoken with that intent. Don't stop her from leaving, he ordered himself. But his hands operated on their own, reaching to stroke her back. She shivered in response.

"Kiss me good-night?" he asked.

His heartbeat quickened with the moment's suspense as she fought a losing battle with herself. The fact that she didn't stand a chance of winning it brought a fierce pleasure. She twisted around to face him and leaned down, bringing her lips to his mouth. Graham lured her tongue into warm, wet contact with his and felt his body growing hard with renewed arousal. He cupped her breasts and fondled them, his motives mixed. Partly he was pleasuring himself and partly he was reawakening her desire.

Holly moaned in her throat when he gently pinched her nipples. "You're turning me on again," she whispered.

Instead of answering, Graham took her hand and guided it, showing her intimately that he was already turned on.

"I thought we'd both had enough lovemaking to last us," she murmured, curving her hand around him.

"We did, for about five minutes." Graham was caressing her buttocks and hips, taking fresh male delight in satin skin and slim curves. He slid a hand between her thighs and used frank language to express his male pleasure in her readiness to take him inside her again.

"Not yet," Holly said when he was about to bring her astride him.

"Oh, right." Graham couldn't believe he'd forgotten all about birth control for a second or two there. He reached to the bedside table, but she was planting kisses on his chest, nuzzling with her mouth and finding his nipples with the tip of her tongue. He whispered her name, flooded by a tide of weak pleasure, only dimly aware that his fingers had closed around a foil packet and were crushing it.

Holly kissed a trail down his stomach. Her hands were laying claim to his entire body, stroking, caressing, robbing his muscles of strength.

''You don't have to—'' Speech suddenly wasn't possible. She was pleasuring him with the most intimate type of foreplay, and Graham had all he could do to withstand the ecstasy. Somehow he managed not to explode into a million pieces. Pieces that would all belong to her and only she could put back together. Did he trust her enough to risk giving her so much control? Perhaps the element of doubt kept him hanging on to a thread of control.

Graham surrendered the packet and let her attend to birth control, causing himself more blissful torment. Finally she mounted him, and the balance shifted. Graham was a full partner in pleasuring her and himself. Strength flowed back into his muscles, superhuman strength, but his sense of touch had never been more sensitive as he caressed her breasts, her thighs and the rest of her body.

She rode him harder and with increasing urgency. They communicated with words of frank passion. They kissed with tenderness and kissed with bruising hunger, tongues mating and lips meshing. Time lost all meaning until suddenly Graham felt a telltale burst of unbridled joy and knew he was at the brink of climax. He found her feminine nub, begging, "Share this with me, Holly. Please, darling—"

She threw her head back, crying out his name. For a brief moment he exulted in the shock waves of her climax before he was broadsided by an enormous shock wave of his own that flung him skyward. Graham grabbed on to Holly and took her with him as he soared out of the universe, beyond the force of gravity. Beyond the reach of reality. He heard his own elated laughter.

Holly was getting dressed when Graham came out of the bathroom. He picked up his boxer shorts.

"You don't have to go downstairs with me," she said. "We can say good-night here."

"Okay." He still put on the shorts before he walked over to her. She'd slipped her arms into the straps of her bra. "Let me fasten it for you."

She acquiesced and he hooked the two parts together. Then he bent and kissed her back. Straightening, he slipped his arms around her waist and drew her against him. She relaxed for a few seconds, but then pulled away. "It's getting late. I need to go."

"There's no persuading you to stay?"

"You don't really want me to stay, Graham. Not deep down. You have your own reservations about us."

"It takes two for a commitment, Holly. I can't provide the faith and trust for both of us."

She didn't answer, but pulled her blouse over her head, her actions and silence serving as agreement with the points he'd made. Graham fastened the blouse. When he'd finished, he kissed the back of her neck above the top button. "There."

"Thanks." Her voice was bleak and sad.

"We have time to build up our confidence in one another," he said, and would have taken her into his arms again, but she moved away out of reach to put on her skirt.

Graham quickly pulled on his slacks and shirt, deciding in favor of accompanying her downstairs. Holly didn't comment on his changing his mind.

Outside in the hallway, they both paused and glanced toward the twins' room. He took her hand and they went together and looked in on his sleeping children.

"They're so precious," she whispered.

"Yes, they're pretty special kids," he whispered in reply. They need a mother and you'd be getting them in the bargain, if you gambled on being my wife. Graham managed not to speak the thought aloud. After all, the situation was pretty damn obvious. Holly could put two and one together for herself and come up with three.

Chapter Twelve

After the taillights of Holly's van had disappeared, Graham stood outside his condo listening to the distant hum of traffic on the Lake Pontchartrain Causeway. The sense of happiness and peace he'd experienced earlier after making love to Holly was gone now. It hadn't lasted long. It probably wasn't a lasting state of mind, he reflected, but just part of the euphoria accompanying great sex.

If this were a romantic movie or a novel instead of real life, tonight would mean something significant. The fact that he and Holly had knocked down all the physical barriers would mark a new stage in their relationship if they were fictional characters. How disappointing that nothing was changed.

They were still two people afraid to trust one another. Afraid to commit, for their own different reasons. Holly lacked faith in the institution of marriage. Or that was her excuse for remaining single. She might just find the flexibility and freedom or a single lifestyle more to her liking. As Heather had.

As for Graham, he couldn't think of only himself and what was good for him now. He was a father and had to consider Jennifer and Justin in making all important decisions. When he married, his bride needed to be someone who believed in the marriage vows, because she would not only be taking on the role of wife but the role of mother.

Permanent roles, in his mind.

Graham wanted the same kind of stability for his children that he'd known as a son. Marriages like his parents' marriage were possible in today's world if two people worked hard enough at fulfilling their responsibilities, at keeping their promises. But only possible if a couple shared a belief in the permanency of their union.

Could Holly ever make the leap of faith that would be necessary?

The soul-searching had put Graham in a despondent mood. He went inside his condo and located the TV remote control, too unsettled to go to bed. As he was about to drop down on to the sofa, the phone rang. He grabbed it up, thinking that Holly might be calling him on her car phone. But the voice on the line wasn't hers.

"Hello, Graham. This is Lena Booth. Heather's aunt. I apologize for disturbing you this late in the evening."

"It's okay, Lena. I was still up."

"How are you getting along with Jennifer and Justin?"

"Fairly well, I guess, considering. We're developing a daily routine. I enrolled them in preschool, and Justin adapted almost immediately."

"Jennifer didn't?"

"No, but she's beginning to interact more with the other children, according to her teacher."

"Well, good. Is she still throwing those tantrums of hers?"

"Not as often as at first. She can be a sweet little girl."

"It sounds as though you've recovered from the shock and are adjusting admirably to sudden fatherhood," Lena remarked.

"Did I have any choice?" Graham asked.

"A lot of men—in fact, the majority of men—wouldn't have taken responsibility like you did. Heather deserves some credit for picking you. But I didn't call just to pat you on the back. Remember I mentioned Heather's cousin, Andy Booth, who was living abroad?"

"Yes. He works for a big oil company, I believe."

"Indeed he does. As it happens, he and his wife, Trish, are back in the States. He contacted me and inquired about the twins. I gave him your name and pertinent information like telephone numbers where you could be reached. I expect he will get in touch."

"Sure. That'll be fine." Graham had no objection to a visit from Heather's relatives.

"Life can be so unfair, can't it? Poor Trish, who's happily married, hasn't been able to carry a baby to term, and Heather decides she wants to be a mother and produces twins. Excuse me, Graham. I have a call on another line." Lena hurriedly said goodbye and cut the connection.

Graham sat there, remembering the scene in his office two weeks ago when Heather's great-aunt had appeared out of nowhere with the twins in tow. It seemed like a much longer span of time than two weeks. Those first few days had been pure hell. He doubted he would have survived them without Holly's help.

Thanks to her, he probably could get by as a single dad at this point. And he might have to, Graham reflected soberly. He wasn't going to pressure Holly into marrying him, and yet he couldn't imagine finding someone else he wanted to marry anytime soon.

Weary of his own pessimism, Graham picked up the TV remote. Before he could aim it and click, the phone rang. "Maybe that's Holly," he said aloud, making an eager grab.

This time the caller turned out to be his mother.

"Did you have anything special planned for the weekend?" she asked after they'd exchanged greetings.

"No, nothing other than going over to Holly's house, either Saturday or Sunday. I'm doing a project for her. A gazebo for her backyard. She mentioned a picnic."

"Would the twins be unhappy about missing out on the picnic?"

"Actually they don't know anything about it."

"Good. This is kind of spur of the moment, but your dad and I would love to take Jennifer and Justin off your hands for a couple of days. We figured you might enjoy a free weekend."

"A free weekend. What a strange idea," Graham said with irony.

"Dad and I thought you could bring the children tomorrow morning and drop them off. We'll drive them back to Mandeville on Sunday evening. We have lots to do to entertain them, including a birthday party for my friend Nora's youngest grandchild, Sarah."

"Justin hasn't stopped talking about the boat ride with Dad, and Jennifer was very taken with horseback riding. They've asked numerous times when we were going to Grandma and Grandpa's house again. But I don't know how they'll like my driving away and leaving them.''

"Take my word for it. I suspect they'll hardly notice.'' Val chuckled. ''They'll be too busy playing with their new pets Grandpa came home with this week.''

"Pets? Plural?''

"A puppy and a kitten. Don't worry. The arrangement will be for us to board them here in Mississippi, but the twins can name them and claim them as their pets.''

"They'll be thrilled, I'm sure.'' Graham finalized plans, feeling slightly guilty over his growing excitement.

Tomorrow night he could take Holly out on a real date. On Sunday morning he could get up and go for a run with no worries about the twins waking up. Two whole days of doing what he wanted to do! He could slip back into the carefree mindset of bachelorhood.

"Hi. What are you doing?'' Graham asked.

"I just hung up the phone,'' Holly replied. ''I called your condo and your answering machine picked up.''

"I'm on my way back to Mandeville from Picayune. I brought the kids to my parents' house for the weekend. Mom called last night after you left and invited them.''

''Oh. So I guess our picnic is off.'' She managed not to sound as disappointed as she felt. A weekend with their grandparents would probably be fun for the twins. And it was important for them to bond with Val and Gerald.

''We can have a picnic with just the two of us,'' he said. ''I can buy some po'boys and bring them to your place. You and I can spread a blanket in your backyard and eat in peace.''

He sounded happier than Holly had ever heard him sound. Almost jubilant.

''A po'boy would be good,'' she said.

''Great. I'll come to your house about noon. One more thing. I hope you're not busy tonight, because I want to take you out to dinner. Someplace that caters to adults. Imagine it. A meal with no spilled glasses of milk. No food scattered on the floor.'' His tone was joking but Holly detected an underlying seriousness.

''I'm not busy tonight.'' Only because she'd turned down social opportunities with the hope of being with him and the twins.

''It's a date, then.''

''You seem on top of the world,'' Holly remarked.

''I feel on top of the world. What kind of po'boy would you like? Oyster? Shrimp?''

"Surprise me." Her light note was forced, but Graham apparently didn't notice.

Even taking into consideration that the last two weeks had been a strain on him, it bothered Holly—bothered her a *lot*—that taking Jennifer and Justin off to their grandparents for the weekend had put him on cloud nine. Just last night he'd been the affectionate, devoted father. She would have sworn that he was starting to enjoy being a parent.

She'd thought she knew his character well, and she guessed she really didn't. Which was more proof that marrying anyone, even a man who seemed completely trustworthy, was too huge a gamble. People were flawed and those flaws eventually surfaced in a marriage and led to divorce with all the emotional devastation and bitterness.

Not for me, Holly thought sadly.

"That was the best oyster po'boy I've ever eaten," Graham declared, crumpling up the butcher-paper wrapping. He picked up his bottle of beer and drained it.

"Would you like another?" Holly asked, dipping her hand into the small cooler he'd brought. They were sitting on a cotton bedspread in her backyard. His carefree mood had proved infectious, and her own spirits had risen. Holly's philosophy was to live every day to the fullest, and she was taking pleasure in Graham's company.

"Don't mind if I do." He accepted the beer from her, twisted off the cap and took a big swallow. With a satisfied sound of enjoyment, he put the beer aside and picked up a sketch pad and pencil.

Holly watched as his hand made quick, fluent strokes and a charming gazebo took form on the page. "I love it!" she exclaimed, filled with admiration for his architectural talent. "It's perfect! Do you always come up with an original design this fast and easily?"

"Lately I've been struggling. It's been like pulling teeth. But today I feel like I could design a cathedral." He tossed aside pad and pencil and sprawled back on his elbows, sucking in a deep breath. "God, it's good to be relaxed."

"The tension has been really bad?"

"Worse than I'd realized."

Worse than Holly had realized, too. She'd thought he was handling his new responsibilities remarkably well, but apparently he hadn't been. So much for her insight.

"Don't look concerned on my account," Graham chided. "I'm doing okay. Right now, better than okay. On a different subject, Heather's great-aunt, Lena, phoned last night right after you left. She inquired about how I was getting along with the twins and informed me that a cousin of Heather's and his wife would probably be looking me up."

"They're interested in seeing Jennifer and Justin and making sure they're all right?"

"I assume that would be their reason." Graham turned on his side facing Holly. He brought his free hand to her leg and slid it up her calf to her thigh. The friction of his palm against the denim of her jeans raised delicious sensations.

She laid her hand on top of his, but he continued to knead her responsive flesh with his strong fingers. "Graham, we need to talk about us."

"Can't we talk another time? Right now I'd much rather make love to you."

"It would be just like last night."

"Is that supposed to deter me? Last night was better than I could ever have imagined." He'd slid free of her hand and was caressing her hips and buttocks.

"Afterward nothing had changed between us."

"No," he agreed. "But I still want you more than I've ever wanted any other woman."

"Really?" His words thrilled her.

"Really." He leaned over and kissed her on the mouth, a lingering kiss that finished melting Holly's insides. She gave up discussion and kissed him back. Whether or not they had a future together, why hold herself apart and be deprived of this wonderful intimacy and closeness?

She couldn't think of a reason.

* * *

"Neat house," Graham said, entering the kitchen without a stitch of clothes on. He'd taken himself on a tour, at her invitation.

"Isn't it? I love living here."

"I like your eclectic style of decorating. The mixture of antiques with more modern furniture. And the faux Oriental rugs painted on the varnished wooden floors are great."

"Thanks. I did those myself."

"I guessed as much."

He came up behind her. She was standing in front of the open refrigerator, nude, peering in. "I'm thirsty. What do we have to drink?" he asked, stooping to kiss her bare shoulder.

"The choice is limited. Cranberry cocktail, Clamato juice and champagne. We left your cooler outside," she reminded him. Earlier they'd been in a fever to get inside the house out of sight of neighbors and make passionate love.

"Let's open the champagne and take the bottle back to bed with us." He was trailing kisses across her shoulders, nuzzling with his lips.

Holly shivered with pleasure. "Back to bed? Wouldn't that be terribly decadent?" The smile in her voice betrayed the fact that she was intrigued with his suggestion.

"Blame yourself for being such a sexy lady." He cupped her breasts and fondled them, his touch possessive.

She got long-stemmed tulip glasses from an antique china cabinet, and he popped the cork. In her bedroom they lay back on piles of pillows in her mussed bed. Holly took a sip. "Mmm. I love champagne. I can taste the bubbles on my tongue."

"Let me taste them."

She offered him her glass and he brought it back to her lips. "Not out of the glass."

Holly sipped and they kissed, mouths parted and tongues mating. "Yum," he said. "I've never liked champagne this much before."

"Would you like another taste?" she asked.

"Please. But I'd better put my champagne down before I spill it on you."

"That would be awful. You'd have to lick it off." Holly wrinkled her nose playfully, her pulse quickening at the expression in his eyes. Their minds were on the same titillating track.

"Disgusting thought," Graham said, his gaze caressing her body as though in search for just the right spot for spillage. He tilted his glass over her abdomen. Holly laughed aloud at the sensation of effervescent coolness dribbling on her skin and filling her belly button. He bent and sucked the liquid and then subjected her to an erotic cleanup, using his lips and tongue.

"That seemed like fun for you." Holly sat up and he obediently lay back. It was his turn to laugh at the shock of chilled champagne pooling in his belly button and her turn to drive him mad. By the time she'd finished lapping up the moisture, he was hard and fully aroused. "Look at you," she said.

"Looking won't help."

"Maybe this will." She moved lower, pleasuring him, which always brought her pleasure too.

The glasses of champagne were put aside and the remaining contents left to go flat as the urgency of renewed sexual desire took precedence, simplifying existence into need. The universe held one purpose for Holly—satisfying Graham and making him happy.

Afterward—she wouldn't worry about afterward. There was only the present.

"That cliché about love and sex must be true." As soon as he'd spoken, Graham halfway wished he could take the words back. He hadn't recovered his wits enough to guard his tongue.

"What cliché?"

"That when you love someone, the sex is better. Different," he added. She'd gone from being lax to being a statue in his arms. "There. I've let the cat out of the bag. But I figured it must be pretty obvious that I'm in love with you."

"You hadn't actually said so before."

"Did you want me to?"

"Yes and no." He kept his silence, waiting for her to explain. "When you love someone, it's hard not to hope that person loves you back. Even if mutual love just adds complication.''

"Is that a roundabout statement that you love me?" He ignored the complication part.

"You know I do."

"So how about saying it?"

"I love you, Graham."

The words thrilled him and filled him with happiness. "I love you," he said, his voice husky with his emotion.

"It's too bad that love isn't enough over the long haul." Her statement was wistful.

"We have more than love going for us, don't you think? Personally I like you and admire a lot of things about you. Plus I enjoy your company. Last but certainly not least, you're great with my kids and they're both keen on you."

"I adore them."

"So let's not rule out marriage. I promise I won't put any pressure on you. If and when you're ready to discuss the subject, we will. Okay?"

Her delay in answering seemed like an eternity to Graham. Finally she said, "Okay."

He hugged her tight, hopeful for the first time that she really might come around.

They took showers and were getting dressed when Holly asked out of the blue, "What's your opinion on prenuptial agreements?"

Graham blinked with surprise. "I've never liked

the idea. Usually those agreements are negotiated when there's wealth involved. You're not an heiress, are you?''

"I wish."

He snapped his fingers. "Damn. For a minute there I had visions of buying a foreign sports car." Her smile was forced. Graham gazed at her uncertainly. "Would you want a prenuptial agreement of some kind?"

"Nothing to do with money. But I'd probably sleep better at night if my rights as a stepmother were protected right from the outset."

"I don't understand."

"Jennifer and Justin are your biological children, not mine. If we got divorced, you might try to deny me partial custody."

"You think I would do that to you and to them?" Graham was dumbfounded and also offended by her low opinion of him. "Your best bet would be not marrying me in the first place, Holly, if you thought I was capable of being a mean-spirited bastard."

"Divorce brings out the worst in people, Graham."

"I don't plan to get a divorce."

"Who does? Yet two out of three married couples split up!"

"No way am I signing a prenuptial agreement

that implies I have to be forced to behave like a decent human being," he stated grimly.

She sighed. "It's all hypothetical anyway."

Graham stepped over several toys on his way over to the entertainment center, where he put on a CD. But music didn't ease his feeling of loneliness. Damn, the place seemed empty without the twins. All of the earlier elation over his weekend of freedom was gone.

The conversation with Holly about prenuptial contracts this afternoon had pretty much killed his good mood. They'd gone to a movie and had dinner at an excellent restaurant. He'd tried like hell to get into the swing of enjoying the date he'd so looked forward to, but he hadn't quite succeeded.

When he'd taken Holly home, she hadn't invited him in, nor had he pressed for an invitation. He'd sensed they both were avoiding another bout of lovemaking that made them vulnerable emotionally, yet didn't bring them any closer to mutual trust and commitment.

I'm leery of putting myself on the line again after my experience with Heather, Graham thought as he mounted the stairs. He realized now that he hadn't really loved Heather, not the way he loved Holly, but he wasn't at all convinced Holly loved him with the same depth. She was an effusive type of person who tossed the word *love* around easily. She "loved" his gazebo design, "loved" living in her house, "loved" champagne and "adored" his children.

In his bedroom Graham stripped down to his boxer shorts. Tonight he could take them off, too, if he wanted, and sleep nude, a habit he'd had to break the last couple of weeks along with a lot of other habits associated with a bachelor's lifestyle.

Graham kept the shorts on, figuring he might as well stick with the new status quo. Tomorrow night things would be back to normal.

Surprisingly the thought didn't raise a strong sense of dread. In fact it brought a measure of comfort. He had responsibilities, and life would go on, whatever happened with him and Holly.

The next morning Graham rose early and went for a run along the lakefront. On his return he straightened up the condo, picking up toys and carrying them up to the twins' bedroom. Yesterday morning he'd left for Picayune in too big a rush to make up their beds, so he attended to that task, among others.

How was the visit at Grandma and Grandpa's house going? he wondered. Had Jennifer and Justin slept well last night in a strange bed? Had they awakened happy? Or were they giving his parents a bad time?

I'd better give my mother a call and ask for a

report, Graham decided. If he didn't, he wouldn't have any peace of mind all day.

Val answered and it was immediately apparent she was glad he'd checked in with her. "They did fine yesterday. We kept them busy, and last night they were tired and fell sound asleep watching a video we bought them. Your father carried them to bed. Then this morning they awoke in an unfamiliar room, and they've been fretful," she admitted. "Both of them keep asking about you and wanting to know whether you're coming here today."

"Why don't I drive over right now?" Graham suggested immediately.

"That might be best. Although we had intended for you to have today free, too."

"Yesterday was enough free time for me to chill out. You can't imagine how good it felt to turn the kids over to you and Dad for twenty-four hours."

"I can imagine it with no trouble," she assured him. "I remember how much Gerald and I enjoyed having a break from being Dad and Mom when you and Greg went to stay a few days with Grandma and Grandpa."

"Did you feel kind of guilty for being so glad to get rid of us for a while?"

"Always. That's just natural. One of these days you'll feel guilty because you're glad in a way your kids are adults, on their own."

"Hey, whatever happened to empty-nest syndrome?'' Graham demanded with mock outrage. He was grinning, cheered considerably by the one-parent-to-another-parent exchange with his mother. This was a whole different facet to their relationship, one that he was going to benefit from greatly.

Before they hung up, Val asked, ''Are you coming by yourself, Graham?''

''Yes,'' he replied without stopping to ponder. He wanted to leave right away, and Holly probably had things to do anyway. The phone had rung numerous times yesterday while he was at her house and her answering machine had loaded up with messages.

Graham doubted he would ever have to worry about leaving Holly at loose ends.

On the interstate he pushed the speed limit, amazed by his own eagerness to be reunited with his children. As soon as he pulled up at his parents' house, the twins came running out, shouting, ''Daddy! Daddy!''

He hugged them, remembering how he'd anguished over whether he was capable of developing parental love for a couple of three-and-a-half-year-olds he'd fathered unintentionally. It had been needless anguish, he knew now.

What he hadn't realized was that fatherly love only upped the pressure on him to become the best possible dad he could be.

Chapter Thirteen

Holly had called during the day and left a message
on Graham's answering machine. "Hope you're enjoying your Sunday," she'd said. "I'm driving to
Baton Rouge to visit my mother and her husband.
Kiss the twins for me when your parents bring them
home tonight. Bye."

Evidently she hadn't foreseen returning in time
to come over tonight and kiss them herself, Graham
reflected.

There was also a message from Lena Booth's
nephew. "Hi. I'm Andy Booth, Heather's cousin.
My wife, Trish, and I would like to come to Mandeville and meet you and see Justin and Jennifer.

We're staying in Jackson, Mississippi, for a couple of weeks. Would you please call me at this number.'' He recited the area code and the seven digits, then repeated the phone number, concluding, ''I would really appreciate a call tonight, if that's convenient. Any time before midnight would be fine.''

Later, after the twins were asleep in bed, Graham played Holly's message again, mostly to hear her voice and try to pick up any nuance that would clue him in on her state of mind today. Was there a forced quality to her breezy tone?

Yesterday she hadn't mentioned a visit to Baton Rouge, and her mother's name had come up in conversation during dinner last night. She'd referred to Elaine Holmes's current spouse, Lyle, as Husband Number Four.

It was so hard for Graham to relate to that type of domestic situation, especially after being in his parents' company today. Val and Gerald weren't always lovey-dovey, by any means, not after thirty-five years of marriage, but their affection for each other was evident in lots of ways.

If Holly were around his parents over a period of time, maybe she would get a more positive view of marriage.

Graham punched a digit on his phone to activate the speed-dial function and ring Holly's home number.

He was geared to leave a message if her machine

picked up, but she answered, sounding uncharacteristically subdued.

"How was the visit to Baton Rouge?" he asked.

"Eventful," she replied. "My mother and Lyle are splitting up. They agree the marriage isn't working."

"How long have they been married?"

"Five years. Mother is moving back to Santa Fe, where she lived for ten years with Bart, Husband Number Three. She wants me to come with her."

Graham's heart sank somewhere down around his ankles. "You mean as in relocate?"

"Yes. My mother is quite a wealthy woman, thanks to the fact that a couple of her husbands, including Bart, were loaded. She plans to buy one of those million-dollar-plus houses in Santa Fe and put me completely in charge of furnishing and decorating it. I could live with her, have my own section of the house, if I chose to."

"Does the idea of living in Santa Fe appeal to you?"

"I love Santa Fe. The architecture, the wonderful art galleries, the climate. And the scenery is beautiful."

Her answer amounted to a roundabout yes. Naturally she didn't "like Santa Fe a lot," Graham thought. She "loved" it. Enough that she was obviously tempted to move thousands of miles away from him, the man she "loved," but didn't want to marry.

"So you're considering it." His voice came out tight and bitter.

"The change might be good. I can't imagine being happy here on the North Shore now that I've gone and fallen in love with you. And I figure you could get on with your life more easily if I were out of the picture. Don't you agree?"

"This is a hell of a discussion to be having over the phone," Graham said harshly.

"It's easier sometimes to say painful things on the phone rather than say them face-to-face."

"It's not any easier hearing them."

"I'm sorry. I didn't mean to end your weekend on a down note."

"My weekend? We're talking about the rest of my life. Holly, I love you, and *love* in my vocabulary isn't a synonym for *like*."

Her sharply drawn breath came over the line. "Your love isn't shallow like mine. Is that what you're implying, Graham?"

"If the shoe fits."

"Damn you! The shoe *doesn't* fit! In a year or two or three when I pick up the newspaper and read an announcement, 'Local architect Graham Knight is engaged to marry Miss So-and-So,' it's going to hurt so much I'll want to die."

"There's a way to avoid reading any notices like

that other than running away to Santa Fe, Holly. You could give up your single life you like so much and marry me yourself. Think about it.''

He cut the connection because there wasn't really anything else to say. He'd spelled out his position: Here I am. Take me or leave me.

And he didn't feel strong enough to hear a reply from her that amounted to ''Thanks, but no thanks.''

An hour passed, and Holly didn't call him back. Her silence pretty much told the story. Graham was about to haul himself upstairs to bed when he remembered Andy Booth's request. Feeling lousy didn't seem like a good excuse not to honor it.

Just on the basis of Andy's recorded voice, Graham was prepared to like Heather's cousin. The other man had sounded like a straightforward, sincere type of guy. Graham's conversation with him strengthened that impression. Andy also came across as very eager to come to Mandeville and spend some time with his youngest relatives, Jennifer and Justin.

''Trish and I thought we would drive to Mandeville tomorrow,'' he said. ''We'll plan to check into a motel and spend a few days.''

A few days? Graham hadn't anticipated that extended a visit. He made a date to get together with the Booth couple the following afternoon after he'd picked up his kids from preschool.

* * *

There was some family resemblance between Andy and Heather, Graham noted as he shook hands with Heather's cousin the next day. A man of average height with a slim build, Andy was fair-haired with blue eyes, but his eyes twinkled with good humor. Heather's hadn't twinkled.

Trish had dark brown hair, soft brown eyes and a sweet smile. Watching her greet Jennifer and Justin, Graham recalled Lena Booth's mentioning that Trish had had unsuccessful pregnancies. What a shame, he thought. Andy's wife radiated maternal warmth as she drew wrapped gifts from a shopping bag and presented them to his children.

They promptly forgot to be shy as they ripped into their presents.

Graham soon felt as relaxed with Andy and Trish as if he'd known them a long time instead of only thirty minutes. The twins might have taken their cue from him, judging from their behavior. Jennifer crawled up into Trish's lap and Justin talked a blue streak to Andy. They hadn't even warmed to his parents that quickly.

The five of them went out to a family restaurant for supper. When the plates were served, Trish cut up Jennifer's roast beef into bite-size pieces while Andy did the same for Justin. Graham was able to eat his meal without interruption. It felt odd not to be the one to attend to his children's needs.

He didn't invite the Booths back to his condo,

although he sensed they would gladly have accepted such an invitation. It was easy to imagine Trish helping the twins with their baths and putting them to bed. But Graham could handle all that himself, and he'd had enough socializing for one night.

Andy had already gotten Graham's permission to entertain them the whole day tomorrow. Graham had nixed the idea of a trip to the New Orleans zoo, though, and not solely because that was an outing he wanted to do with them in the near future. The drive across the causeway was awfully long for a couple of three-and-a-half-year-olds. And city traffic was hazardous.

Call him overprotective, but he just wasn't keen on the idea.

Holly did a double take as she drove past the playground on the lakefront. Those two small children looked just like Jennifer and Justin. They *were* Jennifer and Justin! Holly recognized their clothes as small garments she'd laundered. Who were the man and woman?

With panicky thoughts about kidnapping flashing through her mind, Holly turned off onto a side street, pulled into the first driveway, backed out and reversed her route, headed back to the playground.

The twins spotted her as she strode toward them. They hopped down from a colorful piece of playground equipment that combined features of a jungle gym and a slide the right dimensions for pre-schoolers.

"Holly! Holly!" they shouted in excited childish voices as they ran to her. For a moment she forgot to eye the couple suspiciously. Her delight in seeing Graham's two adorable children took precedence. She'd missed them so much the past three days, missed him. He hadn't called again after their conversation on Sunday night, nor had she called him.

While she was hugging Jennifer and Justin, the woman and man came over.

"Hello, I'm Holly Beaumont, a friend of Graham's," Holly said, keeping an arm securely around each child.

The couple seemed to relax, their serious expressions turning to smiles. "The twins have mentioned you often," the woman said. "You decorated that wonderful bedroom for them. I'm glad for the chance to meet you. I'm Trish Booth, and this is my husband, Andy. Andy is Heather's cousin."

"Oh." Holly rose. The mystery was solved. "Graham said that relatives of hers were coming to visit."

"That's us. We've been here in Mandeville since Monday, more than enough time for us to fall in love with Jennifer and Justin." She glanced at her husband as he spoke her name softly, like a warning.

"Watch us play, Holly," Justin commanded,

running back to the bright structure they'd abandoned.

"Watch us, Holly," Jennifer echoed, following her brother.

"Aren't they precious?" Trish said. "I just pray that Graham will agree—" Once again Andy Booth had stopped his wife, this time with his body language. He'd loosely embraced her with one arm.

"Agree to what?" Holly blurted. A kind of uneasiness, different than her earlier fear of kidnapping, had her in its grip.

Trish looked at Andy. He spoke to her gently and lovingly. "We shouldn't get our hopes too high, darling, and talking about it to other people isn't exactly fair to Graham. He deserves confidentiality."

"But Holly knows the situation. Remember, he gave her credit for helping him through the first week when Aunt Lena dumped the twins on him. Maybe she can reason with Graham, help him arrive at the right decision."

"What decision?" Holly asked. "Somebody please explain!"

Andy sighed. "Okay," he said finally, capitulating.

"We want to adopt Jennifer and Justin," Trish confided.

Holly couldn't say anything for several seconds, although any element of surprise seemed to be missing. Her uneasiness had turned to dread, which felt like a black rock in her chest.

"When did you discuss it with Graham?"

Andy replied, "Yesterday. We went to his office during the morning. He'd insisted—rightly so—that the twins go to preschool for a few hours so that they wouldn't get out of the daily routine."

For more than twenty-four hours, Graham had been grappling with the decision of whether or not to give his children up for adoption. And he hadn't gotten in touch with Holly, hadn't asked for her input.

"What was his reaction?" she asked.

"He said no at first," Trish said. "But we persuaded him to give the matter some deep thought and put Jennifer's and Justin's welfare first. He obviously wants what is best for the children, and he stated honestly that he thought we would make great parents. Our biggest bargaining chip—if such language applied—is the fact that Graham's single and he's old-fashioned enough to believe having two parents is essential."

"Look at us!" the twins were shouting.

Holly transferred her gaze, but her vision blurred with tears of compassion for Graham and tears of deep disappointment. Granted, he was single. Granted, the Booths seemed like nice people and would possibly make ideal parents. Still, Graham was Jennifer's and Justin's father. How could he consider giving them away for what he thought to be the best of reasons?

"Where do you live?" she asked.

"Andy has just been transferred to Houston." Trish named a major oil company that employed her husband. "It would be just an hour's flight when Graham came to visit. We have no desire to shut him out of the twins' lives."

"Of course, you don't know us," Andy Booth said quietly, studying her. He let his question hang in the air, unspoken: *What is your reaction?*

Her reaction didn't matter. It wasn't a factor to Graham, since he hadn't consulted her. Not that Holly could blame him. She'd made it clear she would participate in his future only as a cheerleader from the sidelines. Why should she have input in something so important?

The children had turned their backs, busily at play. Blinded by fresh tears of despair, Holly seized her chance to get away, unnoticed by them.

"Excuse me, but I've got to go." She gulped and bolted for her van, hearing their troubled comments.

"She's upset."

"Very upset."

Holly drove straight to Graham's condo, her original destination. Earlier she'd picked up window treatments for the twins' bedroom from the seamstress and decided to use her key, which she hadn't returned yet, to slip inside the condo and hang the valances. The finishing touch. Now suddenly the whole wonderful project of converting Graham's study into a special children's space might have been wasted effort.

The room might become deserted, a sad testament to Graham's brief stint as a parent/caretaker. A sad testament to Holly's cowardice. She'd lacked the courage to do what Trish Booth yearned to do— and what Holly yearned for just as much. To be a mother to Jennifer and Justin.

Being Graham's wife came into the bargain. That meant speaking wedding vows. It meant joining herself heart and soul to Graham, opening herself up to emotional devastation someday.

For a period of time, though—five years, ten years maybe—she would be the happiest woman in the world. And she was the unhappiest right now.

Holly's thoughts came to a crash as she drove within sight of Graham's condo. He was there! His shiny new blue minivan was parked in the driveway.

Her hands shook as she gathered up the window treatments. Partly with nervousness and fear and partly with excitement.

She rang the doorbell, feeling her heart knocking against the wall of her chest. A minute passed. Holly pressed the lighted button again, harder. She could hear the chimes.

Why didn't he come to the door?

Impatience got the best of her. She inserted her key and let herself in. "Graham," she called out in the foyer. "It's me. Holly."

No answer. The condo was quiet as a tomb. "Graham, where are you?" she asked loudly from the living room.

"I'm upstairs, Holly."

"I'm coming up."

She reached the top of the stairs and hesitated, glancing at the two open bedroom doors.

"In here," Graham said, his voice coming from the twins' room.

He sat on Justin's bed, which was neatly made up, as was Jennifer's. His expression was sober as he gazed back at Holly, but he didn't appear to be distraught, like she'd prepared herself to find him.

"Hi," she said.

"I didn't know it was you at the door," he replied.

She laid the window treatments on Jennifer's bed and went over to sit beside him. "I met Andy and Trish Booth a few minutes ago down on the lakefront. I spotted Jennifer and Justin and nearly had heart failure, seeing them out of preschool with strangers."

"They've offered to adopt Jennifer and Justin." His tone was grave but calm.

He'd made up his mind, one way or the other, Holly sensed. She was terribly afraid to learn what he would tell the Booths. "They seem like nice people, but you're the twins' father, Graham. Jennifer and Justin love you."

"And I love them. That's why I had to weigh every angle."

"You *can't* let somebody else raise them! You're a good father. And I would make a good mother. I'm sure I would. I'll marry you without a prenuptial agreement—"

He stopped her impassioned plea by placing his hand over her mouth. "Holly, I'm going to tell Andy and Trish no."

"You are? That's such a relief." She smiled at him, her whole body sagging as the import of his statement sank in.

He didn't smile back. "So you were saying?" His voice held faint irony and faint bitterness.

"I was proposing, actually. Shall I continue?"

"It's not necessary for you to prevent me from giving away my kids."

"I'm so glad you came to your decision on your own, Graham. The fact that you did gives me a little more needed courage to take the plunge." She picked up his hand he'd dropped to his thigh and kissed his knuckles. "So how about it? Will you marry me?"

"What about Santa Fe?"

"Have you ever been there?"

"No."

"Good. I can show you around when we take the

twins to visit my mother. She'll want me to have a real wedding, you know. The white gown and the whole nine yards. Jennifer and Justin can both be ring bearers. Won't that be sweet? Oh, I can just see them all dressed up in their wedding finery! Can't you?''

He still hadn't responded. Holly was holding his hand and his fingers hadn't even tightened.

''Well, think about it and get back to me,'' she said, rising. ''At least I can hang these valances now.''

Graham grasped her by the waist and pulled her down on his lap. His arms came around her and he hugged her tight. ''You're not going to build up my hopes and then back out, are you, Holly?''

''Oh, thank God,'' she whispered. ''You had me really scared. No way am I backing out, Graham.''

''I was so angry at you these last few days. Just when I needed you the most—''

''I know. Forgive me for being so self-absorbed that I wasn't there for you.''

''You really want to marry me?'' he asked, and she knew he had forgiven her already.

''I really, really do.''

Awe at the magnitude of the moment struck them both mute for a few emotional seconds. Then they kissed, a tender meeting of lips that dissolved any remaining discord.

''I love you so much,'' Holly said, her happiness

bubbling up. "And we're talking capital *L*—italics and bold script."

"I love you. And I wouldn't change anything about you, including your exuberance and zest for life," he added. "Every guy has this fantasy about a special woman coming along, a woman he can't live without. You made my fantasy real."

"That's so romantic, it gives me goose bumps!"

"It's true. And it'll be true fifty years from now, Holly. Do you believe me?"

"I almost do. On a scale of one to a hundred, my trust level is at least ninety-five percent."

"We'll work on boosting it higher. Say one percent every anniversary for the next five years?"

"Sounds like a good goal to me."

They kissed again, and the passion level upped several notches.

"Want to give me a hand hanging those valances?" she murmured.

"Later. Right now I'd rather make love."

"Me, too."

Graham slipped one arm under her knees and stood up, holding her in his arms.

"Have I mentioned I absolutely love this caveman routine where you swoop me up and carry me to your bedroom?" Holly said as he walked toward the door.

"Small *L* or capital *L?*" he teased.

"Small *L*. Capital *L* is reserved for 'I *Love* you, Graham.'"

Epilogue

A year and a half later

"Make a wish, Jennifer!"

"Make a wish, Justin!"

"Take a deep breath and blow hard!"

Graham joined in the chorus of fond voices of relatives and friends gathered around a table in the backyard, giving instructions and encouragement to his children, who were perched on chairs before two birthday cakes, each with five candles.

Holly's mother had flown in from Santa Fe especially for the occasion, bringing with her Husband Number Five, who was actually Husband

Number Three, Bart. They stood next to Graham's parents. Val and Gerald had driven over from Picayune with Graham's brother, Greg, who'd taken vacation time to be able to attend the party. He was acting as videographer.

Heather's great-aunt, Lena, was also present as were Andy and Trish, proud and happy parents of their six-month-old adopted daughter. Graham's secretary, Angela, was there with her three children. Holly's friend Patricia had come, newly remarried, as had a whole assortment of other friends of Holly's and Graham's. There were also several people who'd been neighbors when Holly resided here in Madisonville. Her house now served strictly as guest accommodations for out-of-town visitors and as business quarters.

A dozen or so playmates of the twins had been invited, and all had shown up, each child accompanied by at least one parent. Altogether Graham put the ballpark figure of party guests at seventy or seventy-five. It was tempting as hell to think of making a big announcement later with so many loved ones and friends gathered in one place.

But Holly insisted all the attention be focused on the twins today. And she was right. Graham could always rely on her instincts as a mother. That was why he didn't have a single qualm about expanding their family to five.

The candle-blowing ritual was held up momentarily as Graham relit a candle that had flickered out on Jennifer's cake. Then with great puffs of air, the five-year-olds extinguished the flames. Before the applause died down, they were eagerly asking if they could open presents now.

Holly let the doting grandparents supervise that phase of the party while she and Graham looked on and oohed and aahed on command. He slipped an arm around her waist and brought her close to him.

"How do you feel?" he whispered in her ear. "Still queasy?"

"No, that's only in the morning," she whispered back.

"This is all new to me." He caressed her abdomen.

"Graham, somebody will notice!" she chided him, removing his hand. But she brought it up to her lips and kissed his knuckles.

"Daddy, look at the fire engine Kevin gave me!" Justin brandished his toy.

"Wow, that's neat."

"Look, Holly. Isn't this pretty?" Jennifer was holding up a pink swimsuit.

"It's precious, sweetie! I love it!" She met Graham's gaze and they smiled at each other, sharing one of those intimate husband-wife communications that enriched their marriage. "I Love you," she mouthed.

He knew it was capital *L*.

Graham's life was full of words with capitals these days. New Baby. Soon there would be a New House. They were outgrowing his condo. And kids needed a yard to play in. He and Holly were in agreement on that, as they were in agreement on most things.

As for that trust scale of hers, Graham was way ahead of schedule in boosting his rating. On their first anniversary, she'd given him a mushy card with a note: *Ninety-nine point nine.* He'd kept the card, of course.

It made Graham humble to reflect on his good fortune. He was so damn Lucky, capital *L,* and so damn Happy, capital *H.*

* * * * *

Look out for the next THAT'S MY BABY! *story—*
My Little One *by Linda Randall Wisdom*
—on sale June 2002.

SILHOUETTE® SPECIAL EDITION™

AVAILABLE FROM 17TH MAY 2002

MY LITTLE ONE Linda Randall Wisdom

That's My Baby!

Prim Dr Gail Roberts never thought she'd still be with her gorgeous blind date, Brian, come morning. And she definitely didn't expect the little bundle of joy that was soon to follow!

CONSIDERING KATE Nora Roberts

A Brand-New Stanislaski Novel

Brody had never come across a woman as gorgeous, sensuous, provocative…and utterly irritating as Kate. But Brody was determined to resist her—even though he longed to make her his…

JUST PRETENDING Myrna Mackenzie

Montana Brides

Pretending to be engaged to beautiful police detective Gretchen Neal was the only way Agent David Hannon could investigate the murders in his home town. He could cope…after all it wasn't real—was it?

MOTHER IN A MOMENT Allison Leigh

Runaway heiress Darby White thought she knew nothing about family. But suddenly she was answering gorgeous new dad Garrett Cullum's pleas for help and caring for his motherless children…

SOMETHING TO TALK ABOUT Laurie Paige

Windraven Legacy

Kate realised that getting involved with devastatingly attractive Jess Fargo and his little boy wasn't wise. But then she was forced to trust Jess with her life. Could her heart be far behind?

GRAY WOLF'S WOMAN Peggy Webb

After spending one night of passion with single mother-of-three Mandy Belinda, loner Lucas Gray Wolf discovered she was pregnant with twins! But how would this wanderer cope with becoming a husband and father?

AVAILABLE FROM 17TH MAY 2002

SILHOUETTE®

Sensation™

Passionate, dramatic, thrilling romances

MARRYING McCABE Fiona Brand
WHITELAW'S WEDDING Beverly Barton
FAMILIAR STRANGER Sharon Sala
HERO FOR HIRE Marie Ferrarella
TOO CLOSE FOR COMFORT Sharon Mignerey
WARRIOR'S BRIDE Nina Bruhns

Intrigue™

Danger, deception and suspense

PRIVATE VOWS Sally Steward
HIS CHILD Delores Fossen
HIS ONLY DESIRE Adrianne Lee
IN HIS WIFE'S NAME Joyce Sullivan

Superromance™

*Enjoy the drama, explore the emotions,
experience the relationship*

FALLING FOR HIM Morgan Hayes
BORN IN A SMALL TOWN Macomber, Bowen & Johnson
FATHER OF TWO Judith Arnold
THE FRAUDULENT FIANCÉE Muriel Jensen

Desire™

Two intense, sensual love stories in one volume

HER IDEAL MAN
A LOVING MAN Cait London
THE BARONS OF TEXAS: TESS Fayrene Preston

SECRET CHILD
HIS BABY! Maureen Child
THE SULTAN'S HEIR Alexandra Sellers

BUSINESS OR PLEASURE?
THE AMERICAN EARL Kathryn Jensen
BEAUTY IN HIS BEDROOM Ashley Summers

0502/23b

THE STANISLASKIS

NORA ROBERTS

The Stanislaski family saga continues in

Considering Kate

A brand-new Silhouette Special Edition
title from multi-*New York Times*
bestselling author
Nora Roberts.

Available from 17th May 2002

FREE!

2 Books
and a surprise gift!

We would like to take this opportunity to thank you for reading this Silhouette® book by offering you the chance to take TWO more specially selected titles from the Special Edition™ series absolutely FREE! We're also making this offer to introduce you to the benefits of the Reader Service™—

★ FREE home delivery
★ FREE gifts and competitions
★ FREE monthly Newsletter
★ Books available before they're in the shops
★ Exclusive Reader Service discount

Accepting these FREE books and gift places you under no obligation to buy; you may cancel at any time, even after receiving your free shipment. Simply complete your details below and return the entire page to the address below. ***You don't even need a stamp!***

YES! Please send me 2 free Special Edition books and a surprise gift. I understand that unless you hear from me, I will receive 4 superb new titles every month for just £2.85 each, postage and packing free. I am under no obligation to purchase any books and may cancel my subscription at any time. The free books and gift will be mine to keep in any case.

E2ZEB

Ms/Mrs/Miss/Mr ....Initials...
BLOCK CAPITALS PLEASE

Surname..

Address..

....

....Postcode ....

Send this whole page to:
UK: The Reader Service, FREEPOST CN81, Croydon, CR9 3WZ
EIRE: The Reader Service, PO Box 4546, Kilcock, County Kildare (stamp required)